As The Ceiling Flew Away

Kevin Allardice

SPUYTEN DUYVIL
NEW YORK CITY

Library of Congress Cataloging-in-Publication Data

Names: Allardice, Kevin, author.
Title: As the ceiling flew away / Kevin Allardice.
Description: New York City : Spuyten Duyvil, [2022] |
Identifiers: LCCN 2021056602 | ISBN 9781956005400 (paperback)
Classification: LCC PS3601.L4149 A92 2022 | DDC 813/.6--dc23/eng/20211119
LC record available at https://lccn.loc.gov/2021056602

"An island offers a stage."
  —*Atlas of Remote Islands*, Judith Schalansky

"Today the Director opened his remarks by telling us wh[a]
must always do when the author, the director, and the o[
who are working on a production, leave out things we
to know."
  —*An Actor Prepares*, Constantin Stanislavski

"Bestow upon the eyes of this young couple
Some vanity of mine art. It is my promise,
And they expect it from me."
  —Prospero, *The Tempest*, William Shakespeare

"Conjecture, expectation, and surmise of aids ince[
should not be admitted."
  —Immigration Services and Naturalization Testing ([
Intradepartmental Memo: On Procedure and Best Practi[
Adjustment of Status Interviews, 2.23-464.T-09

This was not real life; this was just a gathering of real-life experiences.

This, all this—the sitting, the standing, the mundanity of it all, the looking forward to the hourly trip to the water fountain as a break from mundanity, the intentionally overindulging at the water fountain because it would mean more mundanity-breaking trips to the bathroom, the miscellany, the etc., the *work*, the work of waiting for the day to end, the work of tolerating time passing, time passing *through* you, the work of just sitting there and taking it, like the still calm image in a time-lapse video—it was all just real-life experience that would one day lend credibility to my eventual return to the theater, my eventual excoriation of real life, up there on the stage.

I was, after all, a dramaturg by training, a bureaucrat by happenstance.

But it was Friday and I was not in the theater. I was in the office, filing. Helping Patricia with the backlog.

I was thirty-three years old, Island-born, and my English is excellent.

See?

I watched a lot of American movies, so.

Anyway. I was a status adjuster at the Island's office of ISNT: Immigration Services and Naturalization Testing.

I'd stupidly asked Patricia if she'd needed any help before I left for the day—I'm nice, see, a pleaser—but then she'd gone ahead and said yes and now here I was finding folder-homes for all these stray documents. I was standing in the hallway along which the R through S files ran, the files tabbed in neon like those at a dentist's office, when Mr. Y. came up to me. His suit vest was starting to strain at the buttons; I suspect he wore it more for its girdling powers than for its fashion powers. His chin was severely cleft, a divot booby-trapped with hard-to-shave stubble. "So," he said.

"Mr. Y."

"Well."

"Yes."

"Hello."

Mr. Y. approached conversation the way a dog approached a warm resting spot, always circling redundantly before finally settling in: "You were born here, right? Where?"

"Here," I said.

"I mean, where here? Like which building?"

"The birthing hangar."

"Right. And you're not leaving."

"I'm not?"

"That was a question. You're not, are you."

"I mean, it's almost five o'clock. Almost quitting time."

"Funny man. Listen." He paused, sighed, an exhale like a performance of an exhale, as if I were a doctor and he wanted me to check the integrity of his respiratory health. But then he continued: "Revenue is dropping. Our budget is under threat. Do you know why?" I gave him the studied look of silently and gravely understanding a problem I actually neither understood nor cared to understand. This consists of a simple tightening of the lips, perhaps a solemn nibble of inner cheek lining, an angled nod.

"You don't know," Mr. Y. said. "I see."

"Issues like these," I said, maintaining a thoughtful chin-scrunch, "they're complicated, knotty, vexing, abstruse."

"Yes, I know you've stalled when you start reciting thesaurus entries. It's not complicated at all. Our population—Arolia's population—it's dropping every day, dropping fast like, uh—well, we're just losing people. And losing people means losing tax revenue."

Mr. Y. had recently been cornering me with urgent conversations of little relevance to me or the particulars of my post. A symptom, I'd been considering, of either loneliness or dementia. It had only been the week before when he'd urged me into his office to show me what I first took to be some sort of spelunking video on his computer, only to discover it was his colonoscopy. ("The doctor said I'm polypless, but I just wanted to get a second set of eyes on my shoot.")

I now, as then, nodded and gave non-committal sounds of supportive contemplation.

"We need to start thinking," he said, "about the ways in which we let people get away." He'd used a similar phrasing when his second wife left him.

"Emigrate off the Island, you mean."

He inhaled, grabbed my bicep. "I'm talking about shoring up our shores. Protecting ourselves from being victims of attrition."

"But I work mostly with intake."

"Right. And I see that's been a real boom industry around here."

He flicked the corner of the manila folder I'd been in the middle of finding shelf space for.

"I'm just helping Patricia."

"When was the last time you conducted an adjustment of status interview for someone *immigrating*, not *emigrating*?"

"Just last week we had the Laskon couple."

"That was eight months ago."

"It—wait, what?"

"I'm attending the Tourism Board's colloquy next week where they're discussing some rebranding efforts. Aim for the youth demographic. We figure college-age Americans are the most likely to expatriate, and now with things over there the way they are, there's a lot of opportunity for us to absorb a disaffected and defecting batch of youngsters from the U.S.—but only if we make our product, I mean our country, attractive enough. There's all sorts of murmurings on social media about people defecting to Canada—it's always fucking Canada. So we've got our work cut out for us, but we've got ideas. Like: if some big Hollywood type made a new, splashy movie of *The Tempest*—boom, suddenly people might care about us again. Stuff like that. Marketing! A lot of these efforts are in the planning stages, so until we can get some of it off the ground it's up to this office to do what we can to hold tight to the citizens that we do have. The Truancy Bureau is cracking down—anyone who falls south of them will be barred from even setting foot off the Island. But for the less extreme cases, it means there'll be some extra work for you to see where we can make things a bit trickier for those with their sights set on leaving. Sorry, that was perhaps a bit too blunt. I need to work on implying and hinting at things. Okay, well, you get it—and you also get that you probably shouldn't go telling people that I said what I said. But —" He looked around, over each shoulder, then back at me, and he mouthed the words, "We'll talk later," as if suddenly worried about being surveilled.

He slunk away and I crammed the rest of the documents under B (Arolian names have historically had a dearth of Bs, as the alphabet the Island inherited had no such belted glutton in its lineup; the B names we do have are Anglicized or imported). From the shelf fell a small Post-It. I picked it up, recognized it at once. It was a note that for years I'd kept stuck to my desk lamp's scoliosis-afflicted spine, a stern reminder: *It is ISNT, it isn't IS*, written in Patricia's EKG-like handwriting. She'd written it three years ago when she'd grown tired of having to correct my reports and correspondences. Immigration Services had recently merged with Naturalization Testing, IS becoming ISNT, but I couldn't seem to, as Patricia had put it, "get it through my thick brain box." I had resisted the change, insisting that although IS and NT were now housed in the same offices, they were still two distinct departments. "It isn't ISNT," I told Patricia, "it is IS." But Patricia kept saying I was wrong, "and I'm tired of correcting your wrongness." She scribbled the reminder on the Post-It and handed it to me like it was a prescription. "Keep this in plain sight, always. It is ISNT now, it isn't IS, not anymore." The Post-It was now brittle with age. I had since accepted that IS was now ISNT, though I still occasionally made the mistake.

•

It wasn't until I was halfway to the University, driving along Hatbrim Road with its uncomfortably graphic signs warning of rockslides and the squish of viscera to which such rockslides could reduce you, that I began to feel the screw of something tighten in my sternum.

I harbored hopes of leaving myself, still, after a decade at my temporary fling of a desk job, nursed dreams of landing on the mainland—any mainland, the prefix *main* suggesting that our little Island in the Atlantic was ancillary to some larger land, when the truth was we'd been unmoored from the start, yet we insecurely referred to all land that seemed somehow mained by continental mass as "the mainland." I still had hopes of landing on a mainland with all my dramaturgical wonder and aspirations, finally discovering the life that had been waiting for me all along. The very idea that Mr. Y. wanted me to be complicit in lassoing other Island-born people to the circumscribed fates of this noble but limiting dot of punctuation in the sea—well, I began taking those blind turns on Hatbrim Road a bit too speedily.

I was on my way to the University, where my old Department of Theatric Arts—in which I'd cut an identity for myself during the simulacrum of college—was hosting a talk by some American graduate student. The talk was called "You Taught Me Language, and My Profit On't Is: Thoughts on a Synesthetic Inheritance." It was that title that prompted my interest in the talk, as I like to stay abreast of all new scholarship on *The Tempest*, especially that which is generated here on the Island, especially that which draws Americans to the Island with the intention to generate said scholarship, as it suggests that the Americans have not yet given up on our claim to history. This was to be a talk by an American woman named Alli Hendricks, and, since the talk was to be held in the Department of Theatric Arts's Arndt Theater, attendance also gave me the opportunity to visit with the professors who'd nurtured my own early flare-ups of theatrical interest—*flare-ups* seeming the appropriate way of putting it, as there was a rash-like urgency and panic about those youthful discoveries of passion. Of course, I had no idea if Professor Ash or Professor Kline would be in attendance, but I could hope.

•

When I pulled into the parking lot of the Arndt Theater, I spotted Professor Ash standing outside in a red vest, a sartorial choice I desperately wanted to rationalize but knew I couldn't, not for this woman who had never worn a shade lighter than pure pitch, so the feeling I had upon first seeing her was the pang of failure, my own.

"Can I park your car, sir?" she asked me. Her face was a painful rictus of professional obsequiousness.

"Professor Ash," I said.

Her face fell. "Oh, dear God."

"Are you valeting?"

"Hello, there. Would you like me to park your car?"

The last time she'd requested ingress into my driver's seat had been at a graduation party some ten years past when I'd perhaps had a bit too much mead and was filled with a bit too much confidence in my own motor skills. "I don't understand," I now said.

"I know you don't. But the world is, has always been, a bit beyond you. Fact is, with the budget cuts, faculty are having to double-duty quite a bit now, and at least I'm not in the laundry room. Lyle developed some sort of skin condition down there, had to be transferred to catering."

She was referring to Lyle Kline, the other tentpole of the Theatrics Department.

I let her park my car, if only to know that the astringent scent of her mainland perfume might be smellable upon my leave later that night. Its fist-clench odor gave me the old college comfort of hierarchy, order, having to answer to someone I trusted more than myself.

•

Inside the Arndt, I took an aisle seat, which I always do because of my nervous bladder. This was my first time back in the Arndt since it hosted that ill-fated production of *Equus* (and while I still applaud the moxie with which they re-envisioned that play with a live nag, the resultant injuries are just further evidence to support W.C. Field's dictum to never work with children or animals), and I was freshly reminded of how hemorrhoidal the sitting experience was in the Arndt Theater, those plush cushions hiding rusty and assertive springs.

The theater was not packed. I worried that the scattered attendees were proof of a deteriorating climate in whatever department Ms. Hendricks hailed from, a dozen colleagues and cohorts trying to sit as far from everyone else as possible, an interesting geometry problem.

As for the talk itself, I was let down. Ms. Hendrick's "You Taught Me Language, and My Profit On't Is: Thoughts on a Synesthetic Inheritance," despite its hook, really had nothing to do with *The Tempest*. I suspect Alli Hendricks knew that her title was a false herring, as she seemed sheepish when speaking it. No, the paper she gave was really about how the early Arolians spoke a language so indebted to cuneiform that the residual pictographic associations shaped our early literature, allowed for a kind of cultural synesthesia that forever saw words as tangible, toy blocks to play with. Interesting enough, but forty-five minutes of such chatter that failed to make good on the allusion in the talk's title had me irked. Maybe I was still twisted about Mr. Y.'s edict.

●

Afterward, on my way back out the lobby, I swung by the wine and cheese tableau. I was attempting to grab some sustenance drive-by-style without stopping, but as soon as I pincered the first cubelet of gouda, the attendant turned around to refresh the plate and I saw it was none other than Professor Lyle Kline, skin still rosacea'd. He was wearing a black version of the vest his colleague had been wearing to park cars, and upon seeing me he snapped to and scrunched his mouth sphincterly tight—not that I could see his lips, but you could always infer their expression from the movement of beard that obscured them.

He then, instead of refilling the platter, played like he was a fellow attendee, made like he was getting a snack for himself. "Leonard!" he said, going a bit Santa-Claus in the voice, the pained benevolence of a shopping mall volunteer. "What did you think of the talk?"

The first time I met Professor Kline, a man I regarded as a bottomless font of experience both high and low, I wound up claiming that I had spent my adolescence living in luxurious captivity after a semi-famous hijacking, lounging lonesomely in a monogrammed robe on the fourteenth floor of an overseas Hilton before finally being released the previous year. I am still unsure where this lie came from, but he indulged my fiction, or rather my need for fiction, and my debt from that now pinged me. I tucked a few more cubelets into my mouth and between tallowy chews said, "A farce. Lured me in with the pretense of more Tempestonia"—as we Islanders call the corpus of *Tempest*-related scholarship that we've canonized with our history—"and I heard not a whit. You?"

Professor Kline's all-pupil eyes shifted to something

behind me, and he returned to his cheese-monger duties, head down, arranging the cubelets into alluring phalanxes.

Someone said, "Sorry about that. Wasn't my idea." I turned to this voice, instantly familiar from the talk but now frighteningly intimate in its new unamplified form.

Alli Hendricks held her red plastic cup of wine as if it were a chalice. I'm not quite sure how she pulled off this illusion, something about how she propped it up in her fingers, elevating the cup's center of gravity from stout vulgar stability to something that needed to be taken care of, seen after.

"Ms. Hendricks," I said, clearing my throat, "many statesiders come here with notions of pandering to our much-vaunted interests. We are savvy to pandering—"

"The title wasn't my idea." She said this in Arolian, though her talk had been in English. "The organizer came up with it. I told her my topic and she ran some keywords through a concordance of *The Tempest*."

I focused on something at an ambiguous distance over her shoulder, moved like I needed to get something over there, in order to remove ourselves—or at least myself— from the audience of Professor Kline.

She followed as I moved with decisive gait to the nothing I'd spotted.

"Still," I said in English, "the intellection on display was impressive, and I appreciate your use of the word 'klaxon' in your little speech. I like hearing new words. It is good to build one's vocabulary. When I hear new English words, I write them down. Here." I began fishing in my pocket to show her the receipt on which I'd recorded the word.

"Your English is excellent," she said. (*See?*) "You don't have the lallation issue most Islanders struggle with." She scratched at the bridge of her nose, freckles dimmed by foundation.

I introduced myself with an extended hand. She shook it, and I felt the recent residue of lotion in the webbing between her thumb and forefinger. "You know, I matriculated here," I said, then realized I was still shaking her hand and drew it back to my own person. "In fact, I did most of my work in this very theater. I'm a dramaturg by degree. I mean, that's what my degree is in." I was suddenly aware of speaking more than normal to a person who had perhaps not invited such detail. "At the moment, I'm not one by vocation, as I am employed by ISNT, the Island's office of Immigration Services and Naturalization Testing."

"I know," she said.

I was trying to determine if the indents in her cheeks when she smiled were dimples or—as they were quite severe—unfilled piercings; Americans pierce cheeks, you know.

She continued: "The valet told me. You do interviews, right?"

I looked over to the bank of windows that framed the parking lot. A bit near-sighted without contacts, I couldn't see Professor Ash, just a small reddish blur amongst the cars.

"Status adjustment interviews, yes. It's not permanent. I will return to my work in the theater, of course."

She said: "I'm hoping to secure a status adjustment, a

green card they call it, back in the U.S., for my fiance. He's an Islander." Suddenly the S-curve of her posture went taut. "Perhaps you can counsel us on the particulars of that process."

And although I know the real-life version of this conversation was much longer, much more elliptical and circuitous, more barbed with scions of fruitless offshoot conversation, and although I know the real-life version of this conversation took place over a few more cups of cabernet, stuttered by the interruptions of other well-wishing attendees and colleagues, I still recall it this way, streamlined toward a simple conclusion, stripped of everything that didn't lead directly toward this simple proposition.

"I would love to," I said.

My name, by the way, is Leonard Nist.

...

There once was an Islander, or so I'm told, who escaped from the Island's one small prison by mailing himself to the States. That's what he wrote on the box, The United States of America. He worked in the prison mailroom and found a plywood box—ominously shaped like a midget casket—in which the prison guards' new rifles had arrived. It was plenty deep, but too short—by about two feet—for him to fit himself into properly. But that's the box he used.

For days after the escape, the warden covered up the prisoner's disappearance. The warden was up for review, and news of such a daring escape would have been detrimental to him. He just hoped the prisoner's body would turn up somewhere, hanged or what-have-you. The prisoner's body was found, but only his legs. As it turned out, he had sawed off his own legs just above the knees, somehow cauterizing the stumps. He had placed the disembodied legs in a bathroom stall, making it look occupied. Another prisoner, seeing the feet below the stall door, the same feet sitting at the toilet all day, and gagging against the rotting smell that buzzed thick like a swarm of gnats around the stall, worried that the stomach flu was coming back and told someone in the infirmary. So a prison doctor came to check on the man in the stall and made the discovery that the prisoner had left his legs behind.

When news of the escape made it out to the rest of the prisoners, hope spread faster than any stomach virus could have, and a riot broke out. Some of the prisoners were able to steal a number of the guards' new rifles. When the riot spilled out into the courtyard, many shots were fired between guards and prisoners. At least one shot was fired up into the sky.

The escapee managed to make it to the States. While the riot was raging back at the prison, he broke out of the plywood box and found himself alone in the Lost Letter Room at a post office in Washington, D.C. There, he hobbled around, opening packages, looking for supplies and anything of value. The postal workers later told reporters that they were shocked when they saw him wheeling himself out of the back room on a dolly, a legless man wearing an assortment of lingerie and jewelry (looking like some crazed gypsy, reported one postal worker). They were so shocked that they didn't even think to stop him. Later that day, after he emerged from a pawnshop—having traded the valuables for a wheelchair, and the lingerie for a pair of Bermuda shorts and a Grateful Dead T-shirt—a stray bullet fell from the cosmos and into his head.

...

That night in bed, Grace beside me, I was trying to explain what Mr. Y. had asked of me, wondering aloud how I might navigate the situation.

"I mean, we're still thinking of getting off the Island, right? One day? The five-year plan?"

Grace said, "Will you turn off your bedside light? It's getting all this glare on my screen."

Grace, her laptop atop her lap, seemed to be perusing a dating website. From what I glimpsed, she was inspecting one profile that claimed its profilee was laid back and enjoyed having fun. She made a noise, "Hmmm," harmonizing with our humming air-conditioner, as if to agree with the man's pronouncements: yes, fun things *are* fun.

Though I'd met Grace as a theater-tech nerd in school, after graduation she began doing design stuff for this online thing, a "news" site that was really just convergences of topical angers, often aggregated. She calibrated the kerning of pull-quotes, searched databases for free stock photos, eye-pinching images tangentially related to content. In lean times, her boss offered to pay her in a kind of cryptocurrency of his own design that he insisted would one day usurp the dollar, so now she freelanced.

"What are you looking at?"

"Dudes," she said. "I'm trying to calculate the average height inflation. If a man says here he's five-ten, could we safely assume he's five-eight? Or five-seven?"

I'd always said I was five-ten, though I wasn't actually

sure, couldn't remember the last time I'd stood against a bathroom wall, put a Kleenex box atop my head and marked its placement in pencil. I was nervous to check now. It wasn't just that I'd been saying I was five-ten all these years; I'd been *identifying* as five-ten. To revise that now would be to revise my sense of self. Five-nine, after all, was the Island average. If I turned out to be five-nine—even five-nine with some eager-to-help but still negligible fraction—then a part of me would disappear into the anonymous crowd of averageness.

"Why?" I said. "Looking for a prom date?"

She flung me a glance, an unconvincing tease. "Look who's jealous."

"Just wondering who'll be joining us, is all."

"This is my new freelance gig. Sorta. I mean, Jill finally wants a boyfriend, a real one, a relationship that isn't mediated by a be-holed bathroom stall like a sheet for hasids."

"Wait. What?"

"It was a thing she did. She said she did. Anyway, she's hitting the scene and nervous, so she's paying me fresh croissants to be her media manager on these dating sites. I pimped out her profile, and now I'm filtering her feed. I have to give her a reader's report on the top five by tomorrow."

Jill was a friend she'd made at jury duty. They'd both been rejected during selection for, as Jill put it, espousing a Hobbesian view of justice. We asked her to be the beneficiary of our spare set of keys, and ever since then she'd allowed herself a kind of sitcom-neighbor access to our apartment and lives. She was a woman fond of the self-done haircut, her blindspots made visible for all in the form of wild uncut strands; she had a utilitarian, be-flannelled style, sneakers and the trace scent of sporty antiperspirant. Jill spoke in a cadence that made everything sound devastatingly witty. She was teaching us a tonal language, teaching us to hear pitch again, to recognize notes, chords, and key changes, after a decade of dry banter had begun to turn us tone-deaf.

"She gave me a list of traits she's predisposed to find attractive," Grace said, "but some of these I simply cannot allow. Self-identified 'geeks,' for example. I've come to the conclusion that when a man identifies himself as a geek, or any variation thereof—nerd, dork, et cetera—it usually just means he has exceptionally poor taste in television, and any intellectualism is simply a cover for that. I like the more outdoorsy types."

"*You* like?"

She sighed. "We're going to have to go on double dates. Do you want to have conversations about American science fiction? We have a vested interest in Jill's mate selection, and I want to ride on the back of a motorcycle before I'm an old woman."

At the moment, I had a kinked sciatic nerve, which made sex a quite circumspect affair. The mounting, the thrusting, the miscellany, had to be carefully calibrated so as not to set off alarms in my lower back. The result of such delicate copulation probably looked more like two marionettes rubbing listlessly about each other, strings tangled above by an inept puppeteer. Still, I made a point of initiating the act at least once a week.

When I had begun conducting adjustment of status interviews, my predecessor had told me that rate of intercourse was a dead giveaway of the relationship's veracity. He meant two things by this: first, that when you interviewed the man and woman separately and they gave radically competing figures—the man always claiming a higher number than the woman, though a margin of error and exaggeration was always taken into account—it was a warning sign; second, that when rate of intercourse fell below once a week, that too was a warning sign. I had no idea where this once-a-week figure came from, but it seemed a good enough standard. Arbitrary or not, one needed standards.

I began making the necessary overtures, Grace whispering "vroom-vroom" to herself.

•

I met Grace working on my final project in the Department of Theatric Arts, directing a play written by a seventh-year senior that involved staging sensational celebrity deaths. While Jayne Mansfield's decapitation was, artistically speaking, the most challenging for me— should the blonde-wigged Styrofoam head really, as both script and scribe insisted, "arc through the air, perfectly mimicking the curve of the proscenium arch beneath which it hurls, hair flowing about it like petals on a posy"?—it was the car crash itself that was, logistically speaking, the most challenging for the tech team, headed by an overall-wearing (and, others insisted, overall wearing) Grace. She was twenty-one, with a saddle of sunburn over her nose.

One day after rehearsal, she approached me in the parking lot, said we needed to discuss pyrotechnics.

"Exploding the car," she said, "I'm concerned."

"Fair enough."

"I've blown plenty of stuff up, just to be clear, but never in a controlled way. I mean, there's something a bit, I dunno, *coitus interruptus* about the very idea of a controlled explosion, you know?"

"Totally."

"I just think we need to give the whole blow-upping thing a test go."

She tucked some loose hairs behind her ears and two days later we drove to an abandoned barn, out where the Island's attempts at civilization began to peter out into the kind of emptiness that now, a decade later, is increasingly filled with condos and outlets of arbitrary want.

After parking on the side of the road, we walked through acres of fallow farmland, the dirt still dry, grasshoppers in the air like pop-flies. The sky was blue and empty, and the air was warm enough to feel in your lungs.

We got to the barn and walked through, leaving rivulets of gasoline, our feet kicking up dirt that got caught in the light slivering in between the loose boards.

Back outside, she said, "Please," holding out the box of strike-anywheres. "I insist that you have the honors."

The matches were white-nibbed, splinter-stalked, and I thought it'd be funny to light the match with my thumb nail, one handed, the way I'd seen toughs do in noirs. But trying to light the match repeatedly this way and failing, little grains of sulfur began to build up in the tight crescent between nail and skin. When the match did finally spark, the crisp flare spread across the tip of my thumb. I pulled my hand back, held it to my chest. The match landed on the dry dirt.

Grace took my hand and quickly stuck my thumb into her ear. The earwax, she explained, served as a natural balm to soothe burns, so they're less likely to blister.

"How do you know that?"

"Just trust me."

And I did. I was standing with her outside a deserted barn with my thumb in her ear, and I trusted her.

"Do you really have enough earwax?"

"Q-tips are dangerous. Might puncture your brain."

When my thumb was sufficiently greased, she gave me my hand back, and I lit another match against the boxside sandpaper. We paused over the way the little flame hopped around in the slight breeze, a head of wild hair flaring around the skinny matchstick body, until black crust curled up past the flame.

I walked over to the puddle of gas, which caught the afternoon light, swirls of color betraying its toxic content.

I dropped the match in.

●

We were both at the University to study the teachable bits of Theatric Arts. There were two different tracks for theater students: the first, performance and playwriting; the second, dramaturgy and directing. I chose the latter, never having the facility for the former.

I'd tried, in my younger days, to be an actor. When I was a child, my mother, an actress herself in the Island's repertory theater, had once dragged me along to an audition for an industrial video about life insurance, primarily because she didn't want to bother with a babysitter, and I wound up making my screen debut at the age of five as the precocious and petulant Child Two, who asks his mom what will happen if Daddy dies. The Mother to my Child Two was not my mother. My actual mother hadn't been cast, and judging from her over-enthusiasm at my casting, I suspected that she was quite jealous. For some reason, though, I had no trouble pretending this character of Mother was my actual mother, and I followed her around the set in the safety of her shadow. It was not, however, the beginning of a fruitful career. In high school, I was cast in a production of *Midsummer* as Lysander, whom I insisted on calling Lysol backstage because I'd gotten it into my head that I was funny, and opening night I discovered my own capacity for embarrassment—embarrassment being one of the things Wriothesley High School drama teacher Mr. Flynn said an actor must rise above (the others being substance abuse and bad posture). Nervous about wearing tights before a jury of my peers, I'd stuffed a rolled-up pair of tube socks into the crotch, which by act three had loosed itself from its moorings and was shimmying ferretlike down my leg. Those in attendance christened me with the nickname Detachable Penis, which was a song by the American band King Missile, popular at the time, and people, both students and teachers, sang it like a fanfare every time I walked into a classroom.

By the time I began University, the extroversion of youth had embarrassed itself into a preference for performance theory over praxis. I'd direct—the director having, from his authoritative remove, more control over performance than either performer or writer; that's what I told myself. And the director didn't just have this control, I thought; he wielded it, brandished it. I liked that.

•

After I graduated—after I walked across a creaking, wobbly stage in ninety-degree heat, after I accepted the rolled-up proof of my education, watermarked, after I walked off that stage and out into the world to dispense my new artistry—I found myself bartending at a theme restaurant near the airport.

I'd tried, of course, to make a good go of it. I sent out applications to intern at The Old Vic Theater in London, The Belasco, The Booth, and countless other theaters in New York. I sent in applications for Fulbrights, to go to England, to Italy, to Spain, to Germany, to Cairo, anywhere really, and I used the same essay for each application, with only the necessities changed, about my love of [variable country's] theatrical history. To no avail.

As I saw friends get spirited away on the wings of their

degrees, to the Continent, to America, to start-ups in Singapore and places that seemed to exist postcard-ready, I began to worry that my dedication to our Island's national pastime had doomed me to reside here forever.

Still, I thought, spending my weekend nights muddling mojitos amongst the festive flair of a theme restaurant provided just enough income to keep my days free and unproductive enough to still think of myself as an artist.

•

The decor of the establishment had a festive beachcomber vibe, more in the style of the Caribbean than our own dour Arolian aesthetic. For Islanders, this was a rather shocking affront to our origin story, so the place was frequented exclusively by Americans on lunch-length layovers. Perhaps my own vision of our national epic had already been corrupted by the West, but it was hard for me to not imagine the restaurant as the little dot of land lost at sea where Prospero finds himself banished: an Island resort, an Island of last resort.

I did not imagine a desk in my future, unless it was a prop desk I would use for the production of *Glengarry Glen Ross* I wanted to translate into Arolian and stage with small children.

But then: late one night, after closing up, I was in the back counting out the till. There was only one other person in the building: Johnny—a spectacularly kind man whose small Arolian vocabulary was spectacularly vulgar (thanks to the line cooks who'd given it to him) and whose Virgin Mary tattoo might have actually been Betty Page (ibid.)—who was cleaning the fryer. It was two-thirty in the morning, and I had just finished closing the bar after spending the evening pouring Bud Lights for three Americans who were fairly distraught that the place didn't have Coors Light, though not distraught enough to not stay all night playing the computer trivia game.

I, in the back room, heard a knock at the front door. Was a late-night drinker trying to get it in, craving a pomegranate piña colada, hoping the place was still serving? I heard Johnny shuffle out there, and I hoped he'd tell this person—as Johnny had told me countless times—to kindly fuck off, but instead I heard, "Yes, ma'am."

I walked out into the bar and saw Grace: my Grace, she of the plaid-painted toenails and decoupage coffee tables.

She was crying, holding a plastic stick vaguely redolent of asparagus-y pee, and was now showing me the little blue cross visible in the window.

•

The wedding was simple, a backyard affair officiated by a friend with Internet bona fides. Grace had letterpressed the invites with small shotgun icons.

Our families met—or at least existed in the same space for an evening. Grace's aunt told everyone she was moving to Iceland because the man-to-woman ratio there seemed more promising. A distant uncle—or a man who'd long ago ingratiated himself into that appellation—incanted what he claimed was, for us artsy types, the real sexy parts from Homer's *Odyssey*, recited in the original Greek dactylic hexameter, but what was actually just the arhythmic scattings of a drunken man with a karaoke microphone.

The honeymoon was short and hysterical, as was the pregnancy.

After a month, when our child turned out to be nothing more than psychosomatic fantasies and constipation, I had already landed a responsible job—to provide some fatherly income and health insurance—at the Island's office of IS (not yet ISNT). I sat at a desk, one that looked nothing like what I'd imagined for my *Glengarry* staging, inputting data eight hours a day.

I was now, somehow, impossibly, average, normal, unexceptional, unaberrational, unanomalous. I had let the current take me.

I'd considered other paths to responsibility, paths that might have allowed for greater wiggle room of the soul: there was teaching, there was always teaching, or so my generation had been told, and I thought, still think, that I have something to teach, wisdom to proclaim or maybe just shout on a street corner. But I remembered my own high school drama teacher, remembered the sad enthusiasm with which Mr. Flynn staged a production of *The Wiz* every year, each time peppering in new allusions to and jokes about American pop culture, and allusions trying to pass as jokes, and often succeeding because of how eager uncomfortable audiences were to laugh at the mere specter of recognition amidst the utter chaos of the production, as with the annual layering of new lines to ostensibly make the play more accessible to the younger (and U.S.-obsessed) generation, the narrative itself lost more and more sense of causality and coherence, became, by the time I was herniating myself in the tech crew, nothing more than songs glued together with nonsensical Steve Urkel quotes and Britney Spears jokes, became less a play than a palimpsest-like history of one man's failure to connect with the youth, with anyone for that matter. And so I kept my desk job.

The health insurance the ISNT job provided granted me and Grace co-paid access to the office of Dr. Luyt, who not only explained away Grace's pregnancy, but also diagnosed her with the Crohn's Disease that made walking away from that new health insurance, and back toward an artist's life, an impossibility.

But the pregnancy wasn't a pretense; it was a manifestation of our bond, I would say—or silently rehearse saying—a bond so strong that it had to appear, if only in our imaginations, as a separate, sentient being. The fact that it deflated in a fart didn't much matter. We'd try, try again.

I rose in the ISNT ranks—not hard, especially in this small office where people are promoted from desk to desk simply to avoid bedsores from their swivel chairs—and, after a few years, was conducting adjustment of status interviews, questioning newly married, binational couples about the colors of each other's toothbrushes before recommending the stamp of citizenship.

But soon enough, I'd be done with all this, back in the theater. This was not, after all, real life; this was just a gathering of real life experiences.

•

It was now morning and Jill was in the kitchen noshing jelly-filleds. Slowly dilating grease spots dampened the pink box on the counter, sugar-dusted tissue paper crumpled inside.

"I was told croissants," I said.

"You look sleepy," Jill said, then cocked her head to the sound of our printer huffing out a page in the next room. "Didn't know your wife was a snorer."

I took a donut. "So you're hittin' the scene?"

"These are better than croissants," she said. "More food groups. From Baby Cakes."

The glaze on the donut had the flakiness of an ancient fresco, and I felt it stick to my lips.

"By the way," she said, "which American slang dictionary did you get the expression 'hittin' the scene' from? Your wife is assisting me to overcome some shyness issues, is all."

Grace, hair in a top knot, stray strands sparking out, walked in—or rather, she scooted in. The new slippers she'd spent untold monies on didn't grip her feet well enough, so in order to keep them from flying off when she walked, she had to slide along the hardwood floor like an ice-skater. She was holding a computer printout, handed it to Jill.

"My favorite is the top guy there," she said.

"His username is Cake4Breakfast," Jill said, jellying the paper with her hands.

"See?" Grace said. "Cute, right? He's American. Plus, a motorcycle."

"Where?"

"In the picture."

"That's just in the background. You don't know it's his."

"Cake4Breakfast isn't the kind of guy who'd misrepresent himself," Grace said.

"I'm not really into motorcycles," Jill said.

"But look at the rest of the profile," Grace said. "He likes music! You like music!"

Jill said, "He just writes: Everything except country and rap."

"A man who knows what he likes," Grace said, "but is still flexible. That's important."

I grabbed the printout from Jill. The profile pictures running down the left-hand side of the page were striated grays and blacks. "You said you'd pick up more printer toner when you were out yesterday."

"You don't have to be into motorcycles," Grace said to Jill.

"We need toner," I said.

"The guy on top is toner than the others," Grace said.

"I'm not all that crazy about toned guys," Jill said. "I like the teddy bears."

"If you're looking for a long-term partner," Grace said, "we need to know he takes care of himself. Taking care of one's body is important."

"No," I said. "Not toned. Toner. Printer ink. We're out. You said you would pick it up."

"Honey, you're interrupting us," Grace said.

"Hey," Jill said to me. "If you find me a foreign boyfriend, there's a chance that maybe you'll have to interview us! Wouldn't that be a kick? That is, assuming Cake4Breakfast here wants to immigrate to the Island. I've heard IS is eager for the American expat crowd, rolls out the red carpet."

"Oh, God, can we not talk about IS for once?" Grace said.

"IS is ISNT now," I said, "and ISNT isn't interested in such political questions."

"ISNT isn't, is it?" Grace said.

"It isn't possible for ISNT to insist on insularity," Jill said.

"It isn't?" I said.

"Isn't ISNT aware of its position here?" Jill said.

"ISNT is..." I hesitated, placed the pad of my index finger on some spilt salt on the counter, licked my finger. "ISNT isn't interested in such political questions. The office is neutral in such matters."

"He's doing that thing he does," Grace said. "Speaking in the professional third person, disavows everything: politics, culpability, even agency. It's worse when he turns himself into a hypothetical: 'One does this, one does that.' It's like he disappears." She looked at me. "It's you, baby. It's you."

I swallowed some donut, said, "You said you would pick up more printer toner."

...

There once was an Islander, or so I'm told, an entrepreneur. After everything else had failed, he decided to start his own driving school. He filled out the appropriate forms, got a license from the city, and convinced a church to let them use their basement classroom one day a week. The classroom was already decorated for the festive joy of learning—the walls painted with an anthropomorphized alphabet, the rejoicing Y and messianic T—but he added his own flair when he got the idea to bolt seat belts onto the desks in order to teach his students to buckle up whenever they got into a car. He employed a ten-year-old neighborhood kid, at a quarter a seatbelt, to hop the junkyard fence and pilfer them from old cars. The kid got $5.25 and a tetanus shot.

The man enjoyed teaching. His wife—who'd supported him through his failed attempts at being a boxing promoter, a restaurateur, a professional gambler—asked him if this was going to be one more thing he could cross off his list of potential talents. No, he said, this was different. He saw driver's education as a noble pursuit, teaching teenagers how to steer not just through the Island's knotted and insufficiently signed roads, but through life as well. This was a primer on how the world worked. His wife just groaned when he told her this.

Nearly every fifteen-year-old on the Island buckled up in that church basement on Saturday afternoons, all of them eager to take his hatchback out for the final road test at the end of the eight-week course. But before they could reach that milestone, a votive candle fell upstairs, igniting one of the curtains. The man's wife was reading one of her fantasy novels in the back pew when it happened, and she saw the flames grow up the curtain like an inverted waterfall. A minute later, Father Dan was screaming to evacuate because Hellfire was coming. Some of those seatbelts the man had secured to the seats were so old that the buckles were caked in rust. Seventy-five cents' worth never let go, and that's why the Island now has no seatbelt laws. To an Islander, anything holding us in place is a reminder of our impending death.

...

Alli Hendricks and her fiancé, Grej Kvint, had made an appointment to come see me at eleven a.m. I'd entered them into the office's common calendar under a designation—*inbound*—suggesting it was Alli who was hoping to secure citizenship adjustment to Arolia, not Grej to the U.S. I hoped that this would please Mr. Y. enough, the increase in population and *ipso facto* taxes and *ipso facto* revenue, to make him not feel compelled to poke around too much in my dealings with them. I could have entered them as *misc.* in the calendar but that would have piqued Mr. Y.'s interests. He was always inspecting things for proof of their essential nature, as he would put it, and so any sign of ambiguity needed to be prodded, poked, beaten with a rubber hose until it clarified itself. Proof, of course, is the nature of what we look for here at ISNT, and so it's natural that, after a while, this basic urge begins to seep into, inform, one's ethos. Mr. Y. had been at ISNT for thirteen years; I'd been there ten. I still had time before I found myself and my mind totally colonized by the organization's tenets.

Proof—that is, in the specific, proof of a marriage's veracity, and, in the general, any evidence of the ineffable— sounds like it should be tangible, like peelings of dermis shed at the scene, gathered and swabbed between glass slides. But we shed proof more promiscuously than we shed cells, which makes it harder to capture and stick beneath the mantis-leer of a microscope.

Proof, I have learned, clings, like cobwebs on a sweater,

yet is just as hard to pinch between thumb and index, examine in the light.

And that's why when one thinks of the job, the job of adjusting statuses, as inspecting physical evidence, as the job description so clearly implores one to do, one might be inclined—one *is* inclined—to think in terms of documents alone. And yes, there are plenty of documents to inspect: not just the marriage certificate, but bank account information, leases, anything showing long-term financial commitment to one another, monetary investment intimating emotional investment. But if the job were simply confirming all those checked boxes, then a machine could do it, and in my office one must be increasingly aware and protective of the aspects of one's duties that cannot be translated into binary code—which was why my predecessor insisted he was an amateur handwriting expert and inspected the angle and curve of every checkmark on hand-filled documents, claiming this was the hidden key to their veracity and could only be done by the human eye. So one must remember that physical evidence is not necessarily tangible evidence. One must remember that when one reads the body and its movements, it is recorded and filed as a form of proof. But of course one might never be sure, mightn't one. Even as one notices the degree to which the man turns his shoulders to his wife as they present their vacation photos—standing, half-huggingly, before the wonders of civilization, or pretending, through forced perspective, to be holding up the Leaning Tower of Pisa, or pretending, similarly, that the Washington Monument is emerging from one's pants—one should note if the shoulder closer to her is raised slightly or lowered. But of course there are other factors in the shoulder-position index, such as the man's natural posture, chiropractic health, even the temperature of the room (and it often was a bit chilly in my office), not to mention the different cultural definitions of polite and affectionate body language. But those things never tell you all you need to know. So one is left to wonder about these things on one's own, things like: when the wife crosses her legs, are they towards the husband or away? But of course, one's large, metal and stubbornly opaque desk might—most certainly always does—obstruct one's view of the wife's lower half, and one must not let one's quest for revealing details appear lewd. For one cannot escape the realization that in giving bodily movements such power, one is inviting inspection of one's own behavior, and so one must appear professional. One must, mustn't one.

"Do you always speak hypothetically?" I asked in my first week of training.

"It helps," my predecessor said, "for one to think outside of oneself. One might go crazy in the first person. Helps to maintain a professional mindset of invisibility."

"Invisibility? Do you mean transparency?"

"No."

•

And now, suddenly, Alli Hendricks and Grej Kvint were sitting across from my desk, smiling. Alli was trying to maintain eye contact while sneaking glances at the detritus decorating my office, while her betrothed was shifting his leg-crossing in a way that suggested indirect testicle adjustments.

"Thank you again," Alli was saying, "for agreeing to meet with us. We were just hoping—you know, we're preparing for the move back to the States, and. Oh, we're engaged. Did I mention that? That Grej and I are getting married?"

"Yes," I said. "Congratulations. And will you be going to—California? Hollywood?"

"Oh, thanks," she said, remembering to smile and twirl her eyes in a bracketed moment to acknowledge celebration, before getting back to business: "Well, we're anticipating the, you know, the interview—for immigration?"

"The adjustment of status interview," I said. "Or will you be going elsewhere? New York is popular, I hear. Broadway."

"We're just trying to get a better sense of what to expect."

"Of course." I smiled at Grej, who seemed a bit startled by my eye contact. His eyes were crawling around my office, found for a moment the thermostat on the wall, the one whose plastic cover had long ago gone missing, the copper coiling of its innards on vulgar display. With Grej's head to the side, I saw the thin rat-tail braid down his neck, a style whose popularity seemed to have a cockroach-like indestructibility amongst a certain class of Islander man. I took this as proof of the immaturity of their relationship; it would only be a matter of time before a respectable American woman put an end to—that is, took some scissors to—that thing.

"It's pretty simple, really," I said. "The interview is just there to ensure that you two are who you say you are, and that your relationship is what you say it is."

Alli said, "Yes, but how do we prove that? I mean, what should we prepare for?"

"Oh, you know. Questions."

"Like—could you give us an example?"

"Well. They'll notice any inconsistencies. Things that might suggest your arrangement is not as you say."

"Arrangement?"

"What color is Grej's toothbrush?"

Alli cocked her head. She seemed about to answer when she scratched her chin in a studied way. "I see, questions of that sort."

"You might be interviewed separately, to check your stories against the other's. How does Grej take his morning coffee?"

"Interesting."

"How did you meet?"

"Understood."

I looked at Grej, whose attention had drifted to my stapler, which was guised as a toy crocodile. "Mr. Kvint, do your conversations often sound like this, like an Abbott and Costello routine?"

"What? Oh, I don't know."

"What's on second, Mr. Kvint. I Don't Know is on third." He smiled, nodded.

I said, "Really, how did you meet?"

Alli gave a friendly sigh, sounding like she was pressing

the reset button. "We met," she began, "on my way back from Helsinki."

She told me about the Helsinki Endangered Languages Project, the acronym of which was catchy and impactful in English—HELP!—but in Arolian was a bit too close to our word for the skin between a man's rectum and scrotum.

Alli had presented her research on Arolian, but did not apparently meet Grej there; she met him on her return to the Island. "I rear-ended her cab when she drove away from the airport," he said.

I leaned back. My chair made sounds like it was cracking its knuckles. "A meet-cute," I said. "What begins with acrimony develops into—matrimony." I held out my hands, framing the two of them.

"No," Grej said. "I'd been drinking, is all."

"Yeah," Alli said. "Me too, actually, from the plane."

"Yes," I said, "but did you hear what I said? From acrimony to matrimony! A meet-cute!"

Grej turned to Alli. "What is he saying?"

"I don't know," she whispered. To me, she said, "So, Mr. Nist, we're really wondering what you think an American status adjuster might ask us, or how they might look at our relationship."

"Okay," I said. "So continue. Tell me the story of your meeting. The car accident. Go on, please."

And they did. They went on. They went on about the little fender-bender. They went on about the exchange of numbers. They went on until about half past eleven. Until: "So, what do you think?"

They wanted my diagnosis. Truth was, I had no say in how my American counterpart would conduct their interview or interpret the results. But they just wanted me to tell them that it was going to be all right, that they had passed a performance test, that what they felt for each other was visible to a third party, legible to an audience. Problem was, I had my doubts. They seemed stiff, almost scripted. When Alli was talking, Grej had seemed to subtly mouth some of her sentences, like a bad actor who'd nervously memorized his scene partner's lines so as not to miss his cue. But, sure, I believed them. That twitch of communication I'd glimpsed in Alli's fingers, for one thing. I believed that twitch to be a gesture of intimacy, a sign readable only by them, but I also knew that ISNT agents—and, I could assume, immigration agents in the U.S. as well, since our guidelines were modeled after theirs—are trained to be suspicious of hands, the way they might communicate between partners to strategize a deceit during an interview. Just as those Hollywood directors of old used chocolate syrup for blood because on camera it looked more bloodlike than blood, real intimacy doesn't always read as such to an audience. But they were in love, and they wanted to set out for the New World. And I wanted to help them.

I said, "I have some notes."

"What do you mean?" Alli asked.

"I mean naturalism doesn't always come naturally."

They both inhaled, held it, braced themselves.

"I just mean there are certain things that people like me are trained to look for. Not definitive giveaways, just things that might make an interviewer push a little harder on your stories than would be comfortable."

Behind them, Mr. Y.'s profile darkened the opaque glass of my office door, like Alfred Hitchcock stepping into his outline in the opening credits of his television program, and I turned to my calendar (which was actually a calendar from six years prior; I'd grown exhausted of buying a new calendar every twelve months so had begun to reuse them on a rotation of a half-dozen years for when the days lined back up), and said, "Why don't we schedule a follow-up meeting for when I have more time, when we can, you know, go through some things, some exercises."

"You mean like an acting lesson?" asked Alli.

"Well, I—I have Thursday afternoon open."

"That's very generous of you, but we're not really in a position right now to take on another expense. I don't know what your hourly is, but—"

"No, no," I said. "I'm just trying to help. Really. So you'll be settling back in the United States?"

They looked at each other in a way I could not read, yet.

"Brave New World," I said.

Grej shugged, or maybe just adjusted his jacket. "'There would this monster make a man.'"

"Ha! Yes," I said, "when they're talking about taking Caliban back. Let's see. 'Any strange beast there makes a man.'" I was so excited by our little volley of *Tempest* quotes that I impulsively reached out for a high-five, and Grej ducked from what he thought was an incoming slap.

"Mr. Nist!" Alli said, ministering to her rattled fiance.

"It was a high five!" I said. I sat back down. Apparently, I'd gotten out of my seat at some point. "So," I said, "shall we say Thursday at one?"

•

Coming home that night, I saw Grace was heading out.

"Have you heard of the Helsinki Endangered Languages Project?"

She tugged on a mismatched boot and said she was going out, to Jill's, to watch that show they both liked. It was a show about people living in New York. Or rather, it was a show about New York with people in it, the same way you'd say a jar of peanut butter, not peanut butter in a jar. The show was about a New York of people. About a place that provided residents with a more shapely identity. The Island used to offer as much, but the Miranda Conference—that is, the Americans—long ago stripped us of it.

With Grace out, I spent the evening watching that show, searching the internet for well-written critiques of it that I could appropriate as my own. I microwaved popcorn, masturbated, cut my toe nails.

When Grace came back, her hair had been cut into a chaotic bob. "It's the Jill cut," she said. "Don't I look spunky?"

I asked what she thought of tonight's episode, prepared my pillory.

"We didn't even watch it," she said. "Just chatted about dating stuff. She's been seeing Cake4Breakfast. He's in love, she's freaked out, doesn't like him. I don't get it, I just don't get it."

She tentatively patted her hair, blindly feeling her way over the new, unpredictable terrain.

...

There once was an Islander, from a different island, who came to our Island. In 1602, when Bartholomew Gosnold tried to lead an expedition from England to the New World, he got blown so far off course that he wound up being the first person to set foot on a then-uninhabited Island. As Gosnold explored this tiny bit of punctuation in the sea, he heard something peculiar. The famous line from his books is: "Where should this music be? In the air or the earth?" Turns out it was a series of whistling notes plucked by the wind as it coursed through a crevasse in the wall-like rock formation that ramparts the western shore. It was for this reason that Gosnold gave the Island the name Aeolia, like the Aeolian harp that he had placed in the window of his London home, which hummed with the breeze.

When Gosnold realized Aeolia was nowhere near the New World, he tried to make the most of it and began hunting for gold. Instead of gold, he found sassafras. Always industrious, Gosnold harvested as much of the root as he could, as he believed it effective in treating syphilis. Time and medical science have allegedly proven that theory wrong, but consider the stats: the Island has always been bounteous in sassafras and (somewhat) free of syphilis. Anyway, after Gosnold's ship returned to England, he published, in 1604, a book detailing his travels to Aeolia.

A typographical error in the printing meant Aeolia became Arolia.

The book was mostly a medical tract about sassafras

and venereal disease, but it also contained some beautiful descriptions of the Island and its peculiar musical talents. The man who funded Gosnold's trip and paid for the publication of the book was Henry Wriothesley, the third Earl of Southampton. Mr. Wriothesley was also a patron of the Globe Theater and presumably the addressee of 126 of Shakespeare's sonnets. It stands to reason, then, that by the time Shakespeare wrote *The Tempest* in 1610, he'd come into contact with the book Mr. Wriothesley had sponsored, and so he surely had Arolia in mind when he created Prospero's Island.

Of course, I know that genealogy—even an Island's—is a game we all play to find some sort of meaning, to tether ourselves to something important: we wouldn't want to be just another dot in the sea, unmoored from history.

We always took the Shakespeare connection as a given, figured it was common knowledge. After all, Caliban's line "Be not afeard; the isle is full of noises" confirms it. (When our little repertory theater company puts on sold-out productions of *The Tempest*, there's inevitably a little crepitation of pleasure from the audience in act three, when some befurried actor gets to say that line.) And when the American poet Colson wrote "Caliban's Blues" in 1947, he explicitly referenced our Island's Aeolian-harp qualities.

But in 1989, this group of academics, calling themselves the Miranda Conference, flew in to investigate our (as they called it, and not un-condescendingly) "claim." I was eight and watched these bearded men scurry around in a pack, like a millipede, a hundred feet and one body roving over every crevice and curve of the Island.

These men made it clear that few people off the Island took our history seriously, that there was another claimant to the title, somewhere in the Bahamas, in the—as they stressed—Americas. When the Miranda Conference published the results of all their sniffing around, saying we had no verifiable claim to being the inspiration for Prospero's Island, that's when President Arndt clamped down on Western tourism and imports.

Though I did well in school, I went about my studies cautiously, suspecting all professors of being destroyers of histories.

It is perhaps this tension with academe—the people who tore us from our rightful heritage—that had caused even our own University to flounder in recent decades. It's impossible for any Islander to see the act of investigating the past as anything other than looking for a fight. I'll admit it might have colored my own initial reactions to Alli. And yet, even though here she was, enacting the very ritual, violent and entitled, we had come to expect from American academics—that is, stealing something that was definitively ours, in this case a person, spiriting Grej off to a more enlightened life back in the States—I liked her, and I envied her mission.

...

Back at the start of University, my decision to pick the directing track came not from seeing *The Tempest* but from seeing the school's production of *Titus Andronicus*. I'd just read the play for a Shakespeare seminar, even though the assistant professor in charge admitted to loathing it. He said we were reading it because it was important to put Shakespeare's great tragedies into context, to understand that *Othello* and *Macbeth* were not acts of immaculate conception, that a younger Shakespeare had tried to till that earth and dug up nothing but rock, turning everyone into comic-book monsters, "rather than staring directly into the chasmal maw of life," he said. "Life, in all its funky freshness, is what tragedy is about, is what history is about. I don't care what the course catalogue said—we'll be reading none of his goddamn comedies, all those fairies and spirits, all that ephemerality. Mark me: tragedy and history are about the horror of existence—fantasy is about the horror of unexistence. In my class, we exist, horribly, sadly, and so shall concern ourselves not with fantasy, but with the pith and marrow of life." He then produced a burp that seemed to surprise him first with its appearance and second with its eggy ripeness. Rumor had it that when he was later denied tenure it was due, in large part, to his disregard for *The Tempest*, our Island's origin story.

The assistant professor's real point, however, was that it was only when Shakespeare matured into middle age that he could fully understand the chasmal something of life's tragedy. Real tragedy, he said, was not for the young. He cocked a gray eyebrow at the dozen pimply undergrads sitting around his seminar table—a challenge, it seemed, to gargle the piss and marrow of life.

I read *Titus Andronicus* and was happy to agree with the assistant professor's diagnosis, that it was merely an immature person's idea of maturity, though I was quietly thrilled in the play's final act when Titus kills the rapists Chiron and Demetrius and bakes them into a pie he feeds their mother. For the first time, I saw Shakespeare as a peer, a teen drunk on gore and gratuity.

Regardless, I went to the play fully prepared to mock it. I was ready to impress my date—a chipmunk-cheeked girl with mentholated breath I'd drunkenly, slobberingly, made-out with the night before—with cutting observations that I would blatantly steal from the assistant professor. (She was majoring in biosomething; she'd never know.) But neither my posturing nor my knowledge of the play's horrifically violent content prepared me for watching act two, scene four, when Titus's daughter Lavinia entered with her hands hacked off (replaced in the production with long red scarves for blood) and her tongue cut out (stage blood drooling down her chin), having just been mutilated by Chiron and Demetrius (future pot-pie filling, I reminded myself), who now leaped around, laughing and taunting her—"She hath no tongue to call nor hands to wash"—and all she could do was stand there in pain, her eyes searching the stage, the catwalk above, the audience.

When I'd read the play, I hadn't realized that Lavinia

continues to be a presence on stage, in the background, silent, throughout the third and fourth acts, before she finally has her revenge in the fifth. I'd read her name in those bracketed stage directions, but since she had no dialogue, her image had never really formed in my imagination during those scenes. Now, however, actually seeing her there on stage, a person, rarely integral to a particular scene's plot, just there, trapped in her own butchered body, I couldn't take my eyes off her, this specter of unarticulated pain, never allowed the purge of language, in such violent contrast to the pompous, hyperarticulate grief of Titus, who lumbered around the stage, an angry gorilla with logorrhea. It was as if her voice had been sucked up by the sheer sound of Titus.

I spoke about this as I walked my date, who'd been talking about something else, back to her dorm. She said, "I don't feel well," retiring for the evening, leaving me to walk home without even one more cool-mint kiss.

•

It was Thursday, one o'clock, and Alli and Grej were again sitting across from me. I could tell they were anxious. Grej was trying for the third time to crack the same knuckle that had already given up all the pop it was going to give. Alli was straightening the iron-crease of her skirt, repeatedly, as if on a loop. They'd been sitting there for five minutes, and we'd been chatting about the upcoming Tempest Fest, but now that chit-chat had fizzled they were waiting for me to initiate talk of what they'd really come here for: specific advice for passing the adjustment of status interview with aplomb.

Instead, I said, "You know what, let's try a warm-up exercise."

"What?" This was Alli who said this. Or Grej. Either or both.

"As I said, naturalism doesn't always come naturally, and right now you're both too stiff to do much beyond murmur lines of rote affection. Stand up, stand up."

They looked at each other as if I'd just asked them to defenestrate themselves.

"Come on, come on," I said, modeling the action, stretching my legs and shaking out my arms.

The two slowly rose. Grej, once erect, looked back down at his chair as if afraid someone would snatch it from him.

"Okay," I said, "first let's loosen up the facial muscles." I motorboated the air, brrrring my lips together. I closed my eyes, moving my head in loose circles on its axis, so I couldn't tell how long it took for them to follow my lead, but by the time I opened my eyes, they were motorboating quietly but steadily. Grej had a dribble of spit on his lips.

"Repeat after me," I said. "Red leather, yellow leather." I switched to English for the vocal warm-ups, figured it would be good for Grej to practice.

"Unique New York," I said.

"New Yeek You Nork," they said.

"She sells seashells by the sea shore," I said.

"She sells she sells by the shnea store," they said.

"Good," I said, switching back to Arolian. "Now close

your eyes, and let's do some mindful breathing to get us centered." (Arolian doesn't actually have a word for "mindful," so I used the English there.)

They looked at each other, bonded in a moment of fear.

I closed my own eyes and began: "Breath in for two, out for three. One more time." I paused my own breathing to listen for theirs, and sure enough I heard the light hush of two exhales, or maybe the air conditioning. "Breath in for five, out for six." This time, I peeked to see if they were following my instructions. Their eyes were closed and they were breathing mindfully.

"Feel your toes," I said. "Wiggle them. Now feel your calf muscles."

With my eyes open, feeding them increasingly arbitrary instructions as I increasingly realized I'd forgotten the centering techniques I thought I'd remembered from Bridget Ash's course, Directing the Actor, I began to imagine myself in *The Tempest*, Ariel invisibly spying on the Island's new arrivals, whispering spells and warnings.

"Okay," I said. "Open your eyes." They did, no longer hesitant, no longer skeptical. Grej rubbed his eyes like a newly awoken child.

"Now turn to each other."

They turned to each other.

"I'm going to make a sound, a nonsense sound, and you're both going to repeat it as fast as you can, together. This is just to get the mind moving, to short circuit that part of the brain that thinks too much, that plans answers and strategizes, so as to reach a state that is, or at least appears to an audience as, more natural. Got it?"

They nodded to each other.

"But, okay, wait. You're still both pretty stiff here. Just, put your feet shoulder-length apart. Good. Don't lock the knees, though. Bend a bit, bounce. There you go. Okay: Babababapooo!"

They shouted, with impressive brio: "Babababapooo!"

I cued them again: "Lalaladeflop!"

"Lalaladeflop!"

"Feedlefeedlefeedletoo!"

"Feedlefeedlefeedletoo!"

"Zappaddapgrap!"

"Zappaddapgrap!"

"What color is your partner's toothbrush?"

This speedbumped the momentum of our exercise and they looked at me. "First thought, best thought! Manamanamanpop!"

They turned back to each other and got back into it: "Manamanamanpop!"

"What color is your partner's toothbrush?"

"Green—red!" they shouted.

"Good! Patapatabooey!"

"Patapatabooey!"

"How does your partner take their coffee?"

"Black—doesn't drink it!" they shouted.

"DodadodadodaFloo!"

"DodadodadodaFloo!"

"Who wakes up first in the morning?"

"She does—He does!"

•

After a couple more improv games, mostly focused on being in the moment and listening, I let them take a little bio break: drink some water, take a piss, stretch the legs. I was pleased with the progress they were showing, and so soon. They were starting to loosen up, their performances less for me and more for each other.

Alli came back to my office first. Sitting down, she said, "Thanks again for all this. I, we are very appreciative that someone on this Island is actually supportive of us, well, leaving it."

I smiled, looked at the door, which was still ajar. Mr. Y. was in today.

"There's one more thing we need to prep for the interview, though, preferably before we actually get to the States, since it'll be so much harder to find someone fluent in Arolian over there. A great deal of our correspondence is in Arolian, and we need to submit a translation of it. We're not asking you to do any work, though. We just need to get someone, a third party, to sign off on it, to say they translated the emails, and that as the translator they are impartial and have nothing financially or personally to gain in Grej getting an American greencard."

"I'd be happy to do a bit of translation work. You know, I—"

"You don't need to, is the thing. We did all that ourselves. It was fun, actually, or at least—helpful." She gave a fluttering smile, a shrug. "If a live performance can't be edited, at least writing can." Then she said, "Joke. So you don't need to actually translate it. We just need someone to say they did. You know, sign off on it, so it looks official."

"I—um."

She turned at the sound of Grej cursing the drinking fountain in the hallway outside my office. To me, hastening, she said, "Yes?"

"Oh. I—would be flattered."

"Some of it is quite personal, so."

"I'm ridiculously professional, so not to worry."

"It's just a signature we need, really."

Someone came in the door, and—before I realized it was not Mr. Y. but rather Grej—my heart spazzed.

Grej quickly sat down so as to hide his crotch.

"Don't worry," I said. "The drinking fountain is broken. It sprays everyone's pants like that."

"I did not pee on myself."

"It's okay, either way. I am impartial. A professional."

●

I agreed to lend them my name, as signatory vouching for the authenticity of documents I had not seen, offered them the authority of my title as a dispassionate professional. And yet. And yet. How professional did I appear, sitting on this park bench the following day at high noon, just staring across the park at the food truck? How professional could anyone look on a stakeout?

I looked down at my clothes, tried to push out some

stubborn wrinkles. I was, after all, there in a professional capacity, of a sort. Since my work with Alli and Grej was to help them perform in their American adjustment of status interview as naturally as possible, to help them forget for a moment that they had the audience of an interviewer, I simply wanted to observe them in a moment when they were genuinely without an audience, or at least unaware of one.

Grej didn't own that truck, merely worked there—the latest in a flighty series of jobs. He hunched in that hotbox, flipping things, wrapping things, handing them to suited men with paper-napkin bibs. Alli had said yesterday that she always met him here around noon, when his shift ended, and they'd spend an hour walking through the park, airing the grease out of his clothes. But she wasn't appearing on the horizon. Not that there was a horizon. The Island had recently become stacked Tetris-like with blocky buildings.

I was hesitant to get too close to the truck, lest Grej spot me. But I couldn't see anything from this distance, either. Just customers, shapeless men absorbing food at face-level.

As I got up from the bench, and began to slowly approach the food truck, I passed a cluster of pigeons who were fattening themselves up with plumage, making overtures of beautiful pigeon sex. Closer to the truck, I could see the cloistered team of cooks, hovering over the grill, haranguing customers unfamiliar with purchasing protocol. Two men inside, maybe three. Grej did not seem to be among them. These men were much too haughty to be humble Grej, too not-Grej to be him. So I relaxed, uncaught in my spying, and stood in line. I ordered a wrap and ate with the other lunch-hour lumpens on a park bench.

•

That night, I noticed that Grace had molted her smell, that familiar blur of sweaty PJs and plumeria, tanged monthly by scented Maxis. The discarded smell I could now only find in clothes we'd neglected to wash in a while, a scarf fallen beside the sofa, socks that missed the hamper and footprinted the back of the closet. In place of that soporific, Grace had taken on a smell that had an architecture of right angles, a smell insistent on invigoration. It came in bottles of neon, sitting stoutly in the corner of the shower.

Before falling asleep, she asked if I'd locked the door. There'd lately been some intruders in the neighborhood. I said yes, I had locked the door. I wasn't, however, entirely sure that I had, and the thought of our home unsecured—the thought itself an intruder in my mind—made me wait until Grace's breath steadied into its sleep rhythm. I then got up and checked the door; after all, almost worse than leaving her unprotected in the middle of the night, was allowing her to fear that I had a habit of forgetting such duties. It was awful what it did to you, love, turning you into a manager of fear, yours, someone else's, the realization that your ability to protect someone is ultimately illusory, meaning you are left protecting, instead, their fear of your failure. In the living room I found the deadbolt unbolted, quietly corrected it.

•

The next morning, I took a shower, and when I got out of the shower my wife left me.

"I'm leaving," she said, standing in the bathroom doorway.

"Oh, could you pick me up some prune juice?" I asked.

"I'm not leaving for the store," she said. "I'm leaving here, leaving you."

I picked the towel off the floor. "I was going to pick this up, promise."

But then she was gone, as quick as a magician pulling loose a tablecloth without disturbing the stemware. I, cold and wet and towel-skirted, wandered the apartment.

On the stove, the teakettle had a torn-off corner of envelope clamped in its spout. Presumably Grace had been trying to steam off an uncanceled stamp. To an outside party, unaccustomed to my wife's habits of thrift, the scene would surely look like the teakettle had developed an appetite, was devouring our junkmail for roughage. Either Grace had left in a moment of impulse—the futility of recovering fortysomething cents from this tiny scrap of paper suddenly boiling into the futility of recovering her life from this tiny scrap of marriage—or it was a long-planned thing, and I was only now noticing the stamp. Perhaps it had been stuck there for weeks, months.

...

There once was an Islander, or so I'm told, who ran a bordello in a little house on a hill that overlooked the docks. She was a magnificently corpulent lady, sitting by the window, clothed in silks that were patterned like the phosphenes that appear when you press the heel of your hand against your closed eyelids. No one could recall a time when she wasn't there, and over the generations when Islander children told tales of her, they focused not on transactional sex but on this lady as an all-seeing godsome creature whose powers dwarfed any Abrahamic deity because the rewards she promised were immediate, corporeal. These children made their beds, straightened their rooms, swabbed their bellybuttons clean of dirt with Q-tips, prayed the Madam was watching.

And then: after apparent centuries as eternal and unaging, the Madam died. This was during my generation. One is always alive for the end of things, it seems. Word spread: the death of a god. *The* God. Who else will judge us worthy now? the children wondered. For whom are we performing?

And then: the police. After the whole Island stood streetside to watch the dozen men lift the coffin into the flatbed truck, the police began looking for the money. The money the Madam had made all those uncountable years. Where had she stashed it? So much searching and no luck.

And then: a wrecking ball arrived. And then: the moment that thing made contact, the little brick house on the hill erupted, an orgasm of money into the sky, for all to see. Those bills flickering ecstatically in the sunlight, the echo of the impact still reverberant in witnesses' chests, the impossibility of the moment still animate in the air, in that beautiful moment before people started scrambling for fistfuls.

...

Leonard of the outlet mall. Leonard of the soft serve. Leonard of the fluff and fold. Leonard in a misspelled name tag and a hairnet. Leonard in crisp brown polyester delivering a box to your door, asking for a signature. Leonard in latex gloves, spritzing disinfectant behind the basin of your toilet bowl. In my office, I was flipping through the job listings in the Island's alt weekly, as was my wont, imagining myself in each position I skimmed past, as was my wont, each one a different way my life could have gone, a different way to fritter away eternity. All these honest jobs, salt of the earth type stuff. What I could have been.

A little later, Alli was sitting across from me, saying "it goes in cycles, doesn't it. Like, a dog dies, its body soon sprouts flowers. It goes in cycles."

"Yes," I said. "So your dog died?"

"You're funny."

"I'm sorry for your loss." Then I noticed: "Your hair is wet."

"It's raining."

I looked up, only saw the ceiling.

"Outside," she said.

"Of course."

"So, I have—" She pulled from her tote a white binder. "I just need a signature. Really easy." She slid the binder across my desk, opened it to a cover sheet. "Oh." She fished through her bag, brought out a stack of tiny Post-Its, then stuck one on the cover sheet next to a blank line. "That's where you sign."

"To say that I can vouch for the translation?"

"Yes. Well." She adjusted the zipper on her hoodie, up, down. "Technically it says that you translated them, but it's just easier this way. It's just a formality. I mean, no one really wants to read through our emails just to—what. I mean, it'd be a huge favor if you could."

"Could read through—"

"No, no—" Her hands clawed the air for a moment. "I mean, it'd be a huge favor if you could just sign it, is all. I'm sure you're busy."

I looked at my calendar. "I do have a dentist appointment soon."

"Yes, so I'm sure—"

"No, wait," I said, squinting closer at the calendar. "That was six years ago."

"Oh." Up went the zipper. "Well, I'm sure it was memorable."

I flipped through the impressive stack of papers, countless emails in sanserif, some long, blocks of text, others short little missives, reminders, loving teases, only long enough to fit on a scroll around a messenger pigeon's ankle. Some featured only a face rendered from misappropriated bits of punctuation, the symbols of language made representational.

"Just a signature is fine," Alli said.

"It's raining," I said.

"It is."

"Your bag is mesh."

"I use it for apples, fruit from the farmer's market."

"You're gonna send it to the status adjuster in the U.S.?"

"Fruit?"

"These emails. Ahead of your arrival?"

"Oh. Yes. I am."

"And it's raining and you have only a mesh bag for fruit."

"Yes."

"I'll get you a plastic bag. To protect it. It's a document, after all, that is important to your endeavor."

I got up, holding the binder of emails, and headed for the door.

"Oh, it's okay," Alli said, "really, you can just sign it and—"

In the hall, with my office door closed behind me, I went directly into the copy room. I set the binder down and unclamped the rings. I carefully hefted the manuscript out, and fed it into the bulk copier. It began ingesting the pages.

My cell phone rang. It was my landlady. I ignored it.

The machine was taking in pages, expelling both original and copy, until—suddenly—it wasn't.

The machine said it was *processing*.

I let out an American curse and pulled out the originals. A few pages were sticking out, half-chewed, from the machine.

I put the crisp pages back into the binder, returned to my office.

When I walked in, Alli said, "I thought you were getting a plastic bag."

I waited until I made my way back around my desk to answer. "Only reusables, I'm afraid."

Alli said, "Listen—"

And that's when my congested-sounding landlady was patched through to my office phone. As soon as I picked up she started talking as if already mid-conversation. "It's okay, I think, nothing to worry about, I think. But, you know, it's my duty to call everyone, everyone in the building, to say that, for what it's worth, and this is not to undermine the, uh, potential danger of the situation, or to make light of those whose lives have been, in the past, affected by these sort of things, it's just to say that, for what's worth, and I know it's potentially a lot, since I really don't know what sort of things you, or the other residents, kept in their homes, but, for what it's worth, the building is on fire. It was struck in that lightning storm. Twice."

•

To watch my home burn—

Even though, I couldn't see any *flames*. Just smoke: diesely, clothy, smearing the building into the evening like a shitty eraser on a shitty blackboard.

Regardless.

To watch my home burn—to watch it disappear into smoke and ash—was to live, however briefly, a brilliant second life: the life of the person I would actually be if I owned all the things that I will spuriously record on the insurance claim. On paper, then, I would come to life, would come to life as a man who—

A man who.

Standing on the curb with the other tenants, outside my burning apartment building, I took stock of the rest.

Here was the elderly tenant from across the hall, her body crushed, tin-can-like, as if subject to greater gravity than the rest of us. Here were the two college girls from the first floor, all soft clothing and hard looks. Here was the super, known to all by a single monosyllabic name—a thump of a name, a grunt, which I'd long ago forgotten.

I tried to match these people to the surnames, the ones handwritten on the inch-long tags in their mailboxes: I knew the lazy curlicues of their vowels, the vague nationalities, dimmed Xerox-like by anglicization, but that was it.

And now, here we all were, brought together, completely pacified by the awesome sight of our home going up in flames. And yet, still not a flame in sight, only dark smoke visible, cause completely obscured by effect. Struck twice, she'd said.

So this is what it meant to be anomalous, a statistical aberration, to be literally exceptional.

•

One firefighter, his get-up looking about as comfortable as wearing a Persian rug, seemed struck by the sight himself, stopped on the curb beside me, to watch. When I turned to get a better look at the man, he seemed momentarily blushed by self-consciousness and covered his awe with a snap-to of authority. Mustache clamping down, he said, "Not that unusual, really. I've seen it before. Lightning striking twice. Or, at least I've heard of it happening. Once, I think."

I wanted to tell the firefighter that it wasn't the lightning, that the team of forensic fire investigators—which must exist, certainly if TV was to be believed—shouldn't search for signs of the first and second lightning strikes, for those blackened-sunburst beginnings of disaster: They should look for signs of arson.

It didn't make sense, I knew. Didn't make sense that a woman would leave peaceably in the morning only to return pyromaniacally in the evening. The only evidence I had was the story of our first date, ten telescoped years ago, when Grace and I drove out to an abandoned barn, and burned it down.

Grace always said I sought closure aesthetically first, emotionally second. So it would make a kind of sense, a kind of Leonard-ian sense, that she would attempt to end with fire what began with it. I knew when my sense of things was being pandered to.

But I still couldn't explain the knotted logic of a relationship whose maneuverings no longer accounted for outside eyes.

•

Shouldn't we all have been freaking out, trying to charge into the building to save this or that prized tchotchke—a porcelain doll collection passed down by passed-on grandparents, faded photos of world fairs attended?

Certainly there was something in there that I should have been risking my life to try to save right now, some souvenir of mine and Grace's shared past, but the things we'd chosen to fill our life with were entirely, purposefully, replaceable. We'd long ago given up the fantasy of shared metaphor, that this or that object could hold meaning for us and only us. Our photos were all we'd invested any kind of meaning in, and they were all digital, didn't even exist on my computer—now surely melted—but on some ethereal cyber smog I'd still be able to access. But, still, I desperately wanted something to run in and save, desperately wanted a symbol of some sort.

•

Before pulling screechingly up to my apartment—or, rather, to the yellow-taped barrier someone had set up halfway down the block as if anticipating the triumphant end of a marathon—I had imagined rushing into the burning building to save an entire lifetime of things, things, things: things that even in my fantasy remained blurred or obscured by smoke; things that, once I and the other residents were finally allowed to wander through the eviscerated apartment building—flames extinguished, site cleared for entrance ("Are you sure this is legal and safe?" "Sure, why not")—to wander beneath ceiling beams both charred and drenched, in order to salvage what was left of our belongings, I realized would hardly be worth remembering even for an insurance claim. And yet, when I poked my head out into the hallway, I saw neighbors with armloads of things, things of such little practical value (was that a life-size Elvis-shaped wall clock clutched in the college girl's arms?) they must have held deep sentimental value.

At the moment, I had only a toothbrush, which I figured I would need, saved from the fire by the stainless-steel travel case that I'd impulsively bought from *SkyMall* while taxiing on the runway years ago en route to some wedding. (Corrugated, I had said; bacteria-resistant, I had said; and not un-dildo-like, my now-fled wife had said, Grace beside me, huddled over a sudoku puzzle like some World War Two codebreaker.)

So I now wandered my apartment, determined to find something I could take with me. The teakettle had held up nicely, though its scrap of envelope and stamp had evaporated. All the practical things—the clothes, the other toiletries—were not only damaged but were unneeded, as I had a spare change of everything at the office for those nights when I slept curled on the loveseat adjacent my desk. And so I gathered the things that looked like they could conduct meaning between loved ones as water conducts electricity: an old blanket embroidered with designs indigenous to somewhere strange, an ovoid lamp whose lava had long ago congealed, a vase striated like a cross-section of sandstone. I set them all in a filing box and set the filing box beside the front door and did one last tour of the place, one last gathering of reflective moments, when I heard something large and load-bearing begin to give way: the satisfying sound of something breaking that was built to break, like the slow cracking of a spine, or a balsa-wood chair in a staged bar-brawl.

I looked at the paisley patterns of burn on the walls, tried to locate the sound, realized it surrounded me, that the walls reverberated with it. Then a second sound joined— octaves higher, rusted—but this one had a frighteningly specific radix: the radial stains of brown and browner just above my head, a patch of ceiling that seemed to go soft, pulse like a fontanelle. I—recalling the earthquake safety film I'd seen growing up on this Island leagues away from any fault line, screened for me and my awestruck cohort by a fretful phys-ed teacher who then modified a game of dodgeball to rehearse the impending horrors of the Big Quake—ran for cover in a doorway, just as the toilet from the upstairs apartment fell through the ceiling, landed in my living room. The toilet sat for a moment, upright, almost invitingly, then fell on its side, splashing tank-water onto the floor.

•

In the hallway, the mustachioed firefighter was shouting to evacuate, evacuate, to leave it all behind. He was escorting all to the window where the fire-engine's cherry-picker was perched to hover people back down to the sidewalk, a demented deus ex machina.

Finally down there, on the safety of the sidewalk—with the landlady pinballing through the crowd of residents, telling us to head to the Hotel Madrid, where we'd be put up until further notice—I realized I'd left behind my filing box of fake marriage props. Or rather, fake props of a real marriage. Either way, all I had now was my toothbrush, clutched talismaniacally in hand.

"That all you got?" the landlady asked me.

"Grace left me," I said. "What do I do?"

"Not exactly the time to talk about a lease amendment." With a honk, she blew her nose into a damply overused Kleenex, and asked again, "That all you got?"

"I have some clothes at my office."

"Best go get 'em."

•

The office of Immigration Services and Naturalization Testing was out in a corner of the Island unused by the youth, an area full of American chain stores. I was beginning to prefer it out there, being able to grab a shrink-wrapped 7-Eleven sandwich for lunch rather than a beef-tongue Panini, Island-farmed. Caring about things like sustainability simply wasn't sustainable, not into one's thirties, the decade when you have to triage passions, hold on to only the necessary ones, the ones that provided your existence with the barest of meaning, and discard the rest, just let fall like litter you hoped no one noticed.

At night, this area was empty, just the fluorescent signs of all-night drive-thrus glowing like bug lights on neighbors' porches.

I pulled into the horseshoe strip mall where the office sat squished between a one-hour martinizer and a storefront rented by the hour to twelve-step meetings and itinerant churches; I had never been able to tell the difference, the bored fervor of attendees, gathered on metal folding chairs, seeming interchangeable. I let myself into the office's anteroom, turned on the lights. The cleaning crew had only recently left for the night; the air's pixelated clarity, from the day's blast of A.C., hoarded inside, was just now beginning to blur, go soft. The sign on the door, handwritten hastily on a rough surface that showed like a pressing in the print, reminded people to keep doors and windows closed.

The office had only been here about fifteen years, but bureaucracy put dog-years on any building. You'd think this one had been here for a century, the way all colors seemed dulled and beiged beneath a scrim of grime.

I knew Patricia kept a fifth of something strong in her desk drawer, and I found it, the label's faux-Cyrillic script promising a kind of Siberian comfort. It was half empty as only a bottle of booze can be, proverbially pessimistic, what remains only pointing to what's gone. I started in on the hooch, felt my insides glow furnace-y again.

•

In my own office, I found my spare change of button-ups and khakis, creased with acute jags from the too-small drawer I'd kept them in.

I sat down at my desk, unlocked my computer with the same password a teacher had first used as a temporary for me back in junior high, telling me I could come up with something better later. As a child, I'd tried to think up a unique, personalized password, pored over favorite books, rewatched favorite movies, hoping to find some neologism that only I would remember, some rosebud-phrase that would unlock the mystery of my own nascent identity. But it proved to be too much pressure, and now here I was, still typing "password" into the password box.

Online, I soon found myself searching names of old classmates, searching for comfort, realizing I was—officially—drunk.

Darlene Charles (first kiss, told me to brush my teeth next time) seemed to be doing her residency at Cedars Sinai in Los Angeles. Jenny Yancey (first boob touch, though I was only allowed to handle the left one because she said that was the good one) was a sports agent representing mostly badminton players. Kimberly Anders (everything else) was first oboe in the Philadelphia Philharmonic, the Phil Phil. Everyone living stateside, all those cities metastasizing to ensure social mobility, or at least a simple somewhere to go. I then typed Grace's name, hoped that the mysterious whoevers who monitor the doings of government-dimed computers wouldn't see this search history as a found poem of impotent loss, hoped that I was safely in a blackout.

•

I woke in my office, my cramp-seized body shoehorned into the loveseat, my hungover brain shoehorned into my skull.

I sat up, put on my shoes. The loveseat was the only concession to comfort my office offered, though it was a genuine one, the beginning of a plan to soften a room that was mostly metallic and wielded a geometrically impossible number of corners. It was a plan that just hadn't panned out.

I stopped by our office's corner kitchenette—drawers stocked solely with the trace elements of meals past, sporks and packets of soy sauce—to drink some water straight from the faucet, and I found a half-eaten birthday cake on the counter, beside it a note in Patricia's handwriting: *Help yourself, but please save the corner pieces for Patricia.* Realizing she'd self-gifted herself a birthday cake as a hopeful but ultimately ignored nudge to her colleagues, I helped myself to a center-cut cube.

The pages the copier had managed to reproduce from Alli's and Grej's correspondences were still in the tray.

In a usually sedate green sedan with a steering wheel recently gone jittery, I drove to the Hotel Madrid, nattering pundits on the dial, cake still in hand.

Our Island's signage had always been comically confused. Which is to say: Despite living here my whole life, I was in the gradual process of getting lost, and nothing alienates you from your own home more than getting lost in the middle of it.

Simply to free my second hand for steering, I folded the cake quarterly into my mouth. When the cake, which had the oddly pleasant responsiveness of a Memory Foam mattress, expanded and got stuck at esophageal level, I had to pull over to choke, gasp, have visions of my sad obituary.

My throat soon cleared the cake, but it took longer for my eyes to clear the tears, and I occupied them with a photocopied email from my passenger seat. The page read only:

the story of Sir Walter Raleigh measuring the weight of smoke, how he apparently weighed his pipe before and after smoking it, then calculated the difference. He was trying to impress his (alleged!) lover, Queen Elizabeth. Obviously his methodology was a little misguided, but I'm sure Queen Liz flamed amazement nonetheless. There was a long-held belief that Mr. Raleigh actually came to Arolia and tried to introduce tobacco to the Island, but of course that couldn't be true since by the time Gosnold returned to England to tell tale of Arolia, or Aeolia, Raleigh was already locked up in the Tower. Still, the myth does have a kind of etiological importance to it, as it attempts to explain the Island's low tobacco use. Anyway, I'm thinking about Raleigh, and Elizabeth, and smoke. And I am imagining him exhaling that smoke, watching it float up lighter than air and then into her lungs, the ineffable made tangible, something that can stain, that lingered long after their lives diverged, in 1592.

There was no attribution. The original, untranslated Arolian was not included in the stack of papers I had. This could have been either of them, or, if one had translated the writing of the other, both.

•

I drove to the Hotel Madrid, as my landlady had

instructed, making a bulbous detour in the otherwise taut route, in order to avoid sight of the old place.

The Hotel Madrid was the only five-star flophouse on the Island. At twenty floors of starched elegance, and a minimum two bills a night, the gargantuan granite facade stood out amongst the corporate B&B's and mom-and-pop motels like Kubrick's stark black *2001* monolith, and seemed to have appeared just as mysteriously and suddenly (us Islanders like ravaging primates pounding at it, demanding something from it, anything—sex, sustenance, cohesion).

In the lobby, the design was baroque, though probably not Baroque, lots of gold leafing, velvety things to sit on. The maitre d's palms were surely as greased as his hair. The obsequiousness of the front desk clerk was shot through with suspicion, but the man registered me under the Fire party, gave me a key cast as a credit card, pointed to the bank of elevators in the corner.

•

In my room, I found two double beds, one bearing the supine body of a man asleep, positioned in a way that suggested this nap was not a choice he'd made but rather something that had happened rather suddenly *to* him. On the unoccupied bed, I set the plastic grocery bag I'd filled with my change of clothes, my rescued toothbrush, and a stick of sports-themed deodorant, the missing cap exposing a soap-stub of glassine blue stuck with a whorl of underarm hair. I was busy applying some of that stuff when my roomie woke, huffingly, up.

Once the man seemed to find a hold on the waking world, he looked at me with that trusting neutrality of the newly awake.

He introduced himself as Baxter, third floor, northwest corner apartment.

I remembered hearing what must have been Baxter's heavy pacing in the above apartment at odd hours, remembered Grace cursing our upstairs neighbor and his restless insomnia, threatening the ceiling with a broom handle but never actually giving it a thump.

•

The apartment building was—had been—at a T-bone corner of intersection insufficiently lighted, vaguely signed. Once a month, more, a crumpled car would appear out front. On my way to work, I would step through arrangements of emergency vehicles. One woman in the building wrote up a petition to send to the Island council, asking for more lights, clearer signs. A woman, presumably, based on the care of her cursive. The handwritten note, the petition, had been scotch-taped to the metal bank of mailboxes in the lobby, a ballpoint Bic dangling from a string. Last I saw it, the petition still had no signatures. I was still unsure who'd written it.

•

Baxter said his girlfriend would be staying with us, that her name was Mel and "she'll be here soon. She's always on time, takes time very seriously. She's from one of those mainland countries with reliable rail-systems."

When Mel did show up, Baxter's posture changed, became something slanted and bowed. His voice inched up a half tone. "Hey, baby."

Mel seemed diffidently slight, slightly distant. I obligated myself to her and her conversation while Baxter showered, and she bounced questions to me surely gleaned from Arolian phrase books, queries about vocation and kin, favorite TV shows. The dialogue felt like a language class exercise; I could imagine the transcript printed on glossy textbook pages, accompanied by contour-line drawings of smiling people interfacing in a park.

What was my job? she wanted to know.

Well, I—

Did I enjoy it?

Not—

Did I enjoy sports?

Sure.

Which ones?

All but the heavily padded ones, I thought, didn't like that armor getting in the way. When the players had protection, it seemed to be cheating.

Meanwhile, her questions kept coming, faster, and as she became more concerned about getting the words and pronunciations just right, she let her friendly and inquisitive tone fall away. It began to feel more like the line of questions an interrogator asked at the beginning of a polygraph test, lacking in curiosity or inflection, designed solely to establish a base level of blood-pressure.

Was I married?

I wondered if the adjustment of status interviews I conducted were equally blunting.

Was I married?

Maybe.

Did I enjoy it?

When the players had protection, it seemed to be cheating.

...

There once was an Islander, or so I am told, who wasn't convinced of the Island's insularity. A wind-dried man, he often stood at the shore and pointed to the ocean and said, "Just a large lake, really. Finite. We've been made the fools of cartographers." Why? "Social control," he said. "Has anyone, really, from a generation within memory, ever wandered the land without the consultation of a cartographer's script? Of course not. What we encounter with our bodies we've been trained to revise to fit the maps. It never occurs to us to revise the maps to accommodate how our bodies actually meet the world they're in. Are you gonna finish that? Mind if I? Thanks." Between chews of the sandwich crusts forsaken by his listener, the man said, "What it takes, what it takes to rewrite the maps, then, is a radical act of the body."

So he trained. He swam every day, hours on end, in the natatorium. He shaved the fur from his body, began to appear pink and tender. He practiced holding his breath for untold minutes. He bought some goggles.

And then, one day, he jumped into what he believed to be a lake, the water encompassed by our land rather than the water encompassing our land, and swam away. This was on the eastern shore, and precisely twenty-four hours later, he arrived on the western shore. Too exhausted to speak, he collapsed. The Island was abuzz with possibility. Had he been right? Had the cartographers tricked us into prisoners? Or had he simply been caught in an undercurrent that took him around from the Island's front door to the

Island's backdoor? If he had woken up he might have been able to clarify, but he slipped away into death. His autopsy, however, revealed a belly that contained the following: three teeth of a Great White shark, a licence plate of Peruvian provenance, an ashtray marked with the American White House seal, Cheerios. He'd been gone exactly twenty-four hours, one rotation of the earth, and when I imagine him swimming, I see him staying exactly still at his point in space, sundry land masses be damned, while the globe turned treadmill-like beneath him.

...

I awoke to the clotted sounds of discreet fucking in the neighboring bed, muffled hushings and courteously shortened thrustings. My back to the fuckers, I fumbled in the faint clock-light for earplugs, spongy missile-y things, hot pink. With them inserted, my heartbeat and breath felt amplified in the chamber acoustics of my skull, the coitus reduced to breezily distant ruffles, mere static.

Intimacy, that's what I'd been trained to call, in all official government correspondences, the act of fucking. And yet, for reasons I'd never understood, I was never supposed to use it as an adjective: I had to freeze it as a noun. Couples were never intimate; they always had intimacy: possessed it, held on to it. In the status adjustment reports my predecessor wrote—which I'd pored over and continued to reference as a kind of style manual for my own reports—the word was always capitalized, as if an allegorical pronoun. I could imagine the character of Intimacy slinking across the stage in a medieval morality play, a con artist, cloaked in velour, the mouth of its mask forming an O, either out of shock or imitating the fellatiously inviting mouth of a blowup doll, you never could be sure. At this thought, I realized I was probably asleep again.

But then, I was awake again, searching in the starchy sheet-folds for the earplugs.

"You snore funny." It was Mel, standing at the foot of my bed, wrapped in towels monogrammed for a different hotel.

"It's a sinus issue."

"Baxter said it is like the snore of Big Bird."

"I've heard that before."

"Birds do not snore. They lack both uvulas and soft palates."

"I didn't know that."

"Baxter thought that you were awake. He thought you were faking the snore in order to watch us. Which is how come he did it harder than he does normally. He's like that. He videos us sometimes, puts it online."

I peeled myself out of the sheets, held tight to one corner to conceal a stupidly hopeful boner: as if it hadn't got the news.

"So what are your plans for the day?" she asked.

"I'm going to find my wife," I said. Grace had always said the thing keeping me in my job was a simple fear of assertion. Even in those college plays, she'd said, I muted confrontation. So there, *going to find my wife*, a thesis statement, a declaration of purpose, so simple and direct it was almost embarrassing. ("You can play a different character with those not overly familiar with the language," my predecessor had said. "Their standards of judgement are different.")

"Try the Internet," Mel said. "Lots of good wives there."

I folded myself into my pants.

"That's where Baxter and I found each other." She was watching me dress without the usual Puritan averting of the eyes that most Islanders had cultivated. "But he tells people he found me at a bar. We'll go to Paris for our honeymoon. Romantic. Have you been to romantic Paris?"

"On my honeymoon, actually."

"And it was romantic." She nodded as if she were feeding me my line.

Baxter came out of the bathroom, plumes of shower steam cushioning his entrance like smoke in a magic show. He strutted around the room as if on a catwalk, finally came to first position beside giggling Mel.

"See, Leonard?" Mel said. "That is what you need to find a wife, confidence and humor."

"Who's looking for a wife?" Baxter asked me. He switched into English and in doing so, as was common amongst our generation of Islanders, switched into a posture torqued more toward confidence. As Baxter gave me advice on finding a wife, Mel mouthed his words, a half-second behind, a visual echo, a bad dubbing; she was learning the shapes of the words, the way a mouth carves them out of air, sets them loose.

•

The story, as I had told it, was this: Honeymooning in Paris, while Grace shopped in the Sixth, I took a twenty-euro cruise down the Seine. While my fellow sightseers sat in the rows of pew-like seats, sipped glasses of rosé-and-ice-cubes, passively letting the city's sights float past, I stood at the prow of the great vessel, awake, alive, sensitive to all stimuli, the literal man in the boat reclaiming my confidence after a fruitless night failing the proverbial man in the boat, now aiming Grace's Nikon digital zoom at the Louvre, Notre

Dame, Shakespeare and Co., young Parisians drinking from bottles on the bank—excited to recognize images from postcards and take postcard-like photos of them, while also being frustrated by their relentless photogenicity, as if tourism was just a confirmation process, a vetting of authenticity in 30 SPF and cargo shorts—when, just as we were passing beneath the *Pont des Arts*, I felt a sharp ping on my head, then heard a little metallic clank down by my feet. It was a key, there on the crosshatch-embossed metal deck. I picked it up. A little key, it was modestly toothed and shiny new, too big for a diary, too small for a house. Perhaps this key belonged to a fellow vacationer who'd failed to notice it slipping from his lanyard while he gazed down the famous river. At the next stop, I disembarked and walked back to the *pont* in search of a worried traveler with a keyless lanyard round his neck. Instead, I found a pedestrian bridge ornamented with millions of padlocks, cluttered and dense as armor, each one inscribed with the name of a couple ampersanded together for eternity, or at least until a guy with a bolt-cutter came by. At the crest of the bridge, a dozen feet away, a man and a woman—middle-aged, fanny-packed and wine-flushed—added another lock to the collection, kissed, tossed their key into the river. I looked at the key in my hand, and considered chucking it into the water like its owners had intended, but I hesitated. It felt good to hold it, to feel the utilitarian trinket transform back into something symbolic. Like keeping someone else's secret, I wanted to hold it to myself forever and show it off to everyone at the same time. For the remainder of the trip,

I kept thinking I would return to the Seine and toss it into the river, but before I knew it, I was back home and the thing was not in the river; it was on my desk. And every time I looked at it, I imagined the couple—their faces pixelated in anonymity—who'd watched the orange sun setting at the tip of the Louvre Pyramid before locking their love together and throwing away, or at least thinking they were throwing away, the key.

It wasn't until I actually visited Paris, long after I'd begun telling this story, that I realized I'd imagined the scene all wrong. Standing on the *Pont des Arts*, the sun would set opposite the Louvre Pyramid, which wasn't even visible from the bridge. But it made no difference, not really. I'd been telling it like that—at dinner parties, holiday gatherings, to myself in idle moments—as a way of transforming the strange nature of my work into something purely anecdotal. All the details I'd used in the story I'd gotten from my predecessor, who'd told me that story about the little key, which had been hanging from a string on his desk lamp, and I figured my predecessor probably hadn't actually been to Paris either, had simply heard about so-called "love locks" during one of his adjustment of status interviews and concocted the whole thing just so he could conclude by pincering the key and saying, "We are holders of others' secrets."

•

We did go to Paris, Grace and I, though not on honeymoon.

Our actual honeymoon, as it happened, was a traffic-clotted trip to the coast, a cabinned night drinking the bottle of mead an uncle had gifted us, because, according to the man's hastily written card, honeymoons were so named because you had to give bride and groom enough honey wine to last a month. We finished the bottle in one storm-frayed night and drove home swaddled in hangovers that felt like fiberglass insulation in our skulls.

The Paris trip, though, was merely opportunistic, made possible by a great aunt of attritioning years doling out air-miles from her credit card.

Having both stage-handed a ham-fisted production of *Les Mis* in college, Grace and I dreamed dreams of visiting the Victor Hugo house.

The house's preserved living quarters were not unlike the maquette showrooms of a home furnishing store, already halved as if on stage. There were a lot of dinner plates hanging from the walls—recreating the style of the time or compensating for the tour's eschewing of the kitchen, we weren't sure. I, in my flailing French—which had gathered the affected accent of our dear old prof Bridget Ash, that gaunt neorealist who pronounced "genre" and "bourgeois" as if they were pastries she did not care for—read a plaque about Hugo's daughter who "drowned her lover." Over a lunch of Nescafe and McCamemberts, Grace and I wondered aloud about such a gruesome story—the whys, the hows, the holy-fucks. By the time we returned to our hotel, the story had reached Court TV proportions of scandal, only for us to fact-check it and discover that my translation had left out the "with," had omitted the all-important "avec." Leopoldine Hugo drowned *with* her lover. Suddenly it was no longer a story that needed expanding and investigating. It was, had always been, devastatingly complete on that plaque.

•

One day, I was driving home from the office; that is, I was driving to the Madrid, at which I'd been living long enough (a week, maybe?) for the route to feel automatic. I turned onto Main Street and stopped.

Traffic was at a stand-still. In front of me, a child was playing in the back of a station wagon and started idly banging his head against the window until the driver turned around and scolded him.

I pressed the seesaw button on my armrest and my window buzzed down. I stuck my head out the window like a dog, trying to get a better look at the obstruction, and that's when I noticed the helicopters overhead, circling like carrion birds. They were all emblazoned with letters and numbers of our local news outlets. All those chopper blades making puree of the afternoon air.

Surely something had happened, something big, something tragic. Something big and exciting that had nothing to do with me.

Maybe people turning on the TV right now were seeing the Island cracked open and displayed to the world like a geode.

I looked up at the helicopters, gave a wave, then tucked my head back into the car.

Across the sidewalk was a half-filled parking lot for a vacant storefront, so, with little hope that this mess would clear before sundown, I yanked the steering wheel and accelerated right over—*bu-bump*—the sidewalk—*bu-bump*—and into the parking lot, only thinking to check for pedestrians after the fact. I'd come back for the car after this apocalypse had calmed down a bit.

My Volvo's front grille had fallen off years ago, exposing the radiator fan like a propeller, as if this unaerodynamic thing could defy its augury, just take off into the atmosphere.

I walked down the sidewalk, passing all those cars, those little snow-globes of frustration, people revving their engines in impotent neutral. One driver, a man in a sensible minivan, appeared to be crying. Another seemed to be doing paperwork. Another man had binoculars and was studying the upper-story windows of the flanking buildings. I glanced up there myself but found no silhouetted nudes.

The sounds up ahead pulled me on, and I could see the edge of the Something that had Happened. A news van with some sort of satellite space-needle propped up on top was parked where the sidewalk paused for an alley. The sliding door was open and two guys in shirt-sleeves were relaxing inside, as if taking a break from being interested. A cop car was angled obliquely next to it, its snout sticking out into the street.

When I approached the van, a cop walked up, giving jazz hands, saying, "Not this way."

"What's going on here?"

"Tempest Fest, of course!"

Of course, Tempest Fest—our biannual celebration of our Island's origin story, everyone in costumes of the characters, countless productions on every street corner. It was always impossible to tell when the Tempest Fest would actually happen; everyone on the committee agreed that the Constitution dictated it be biannual, but there were factions split over the exact meaning of "biannual": some saying it meant twice a year, others saying once every two years, the practice entirely dependent upon which party happened to be in power that particular year.

"We need to close car traffic for them to set up the big top tent."

"But I'm just walking," I said. "I'm not driving."

The cop considered this. "Go ahead," he said, waving me through.

So I kept walking, past a paddy wagon, parked, doors open, the interior like a safe deposit box. Another cop was standing just outside, playing a solo game of handball, flinging a tennis ball in, letting it describe some Pythagorean theorem against the walls and floor, then bounce back out to him. I hadn't realized how rowdy these Fests had been getting.

•

I heard, amidst the industrial din of stalled traffic, someone calling my name. I stopped and looked around, back down the block, up the line of cars, suddenly conscious of how paranoid I must have looked. Then I saw a pale arm waving from a little Geo Metro. I remembered joking with Penny that she drove a golf ball; not only was the car white and economically spherical, it had been scalloped with a thousand dents from the stonelike berries that fell every autumn from the tree overhanging her parking spot.

"Yoo-hoo," she called. "Leonard, over here."

Penny was another theater major from my University days. For the first few years after graduation, she'd regularly move to the States, to New York, with much to-do—always throwing a farewell party at a beer garden where she'd drunkenly mangle Henry Five's "Once more unto the breach" speech while pointing a kabob swordlike toward the direction she figured Broadway to be—and then months later slink back to the Island without a peep, quiet as a kitten. These last five years she'd stayed put, though still spoke rhapsodically about her days in the Apple. And now here she was, waving that arm of hers as if doing semaphore on a runway tarmac, her voice somersaulting and cheery. I waved, smiled, said hey—in that robotic order, too deliberate to look natural.

As I approached, I saw that she looked different somehow. The hair. She'd cut it, banged it, dyed it even darker, crisp and black.

"Leonard," she said. "You should have seen your face there on the sidewalk. It was too funny. You looked like one of those kids at a spelling bee, trying to think of how to spell 'autochthonous.'"

"Sorry," I said. "I'm just a little distracted."

"Can't blame you. It's like the Pope's coming to town or something. I thought this was every other year. Either way, it seems to get worse each time, like global warming, or a mole you're trying to ignore. Get in. I'll give you a ride to nowhere."

I always liked riding shotgun in her little car; it made me feel tall. I once again bundled my legs up in front of me, the position of the seatback feeling awfully ergonomic. Her gearshift was wearing a scrunchie like a tutu.

"So," she said, "let's palaver. Fill me in. Where are you going, where have you been? You and Grace finally ditching adulthood and doing something big? Are you going to mount the *Henriad* in a parking lot? What are your big plans for world domination? Staging Beckett's *Not I* with a ball gag?"

She'd mastered the art of sounding sincere and condescending at the same time.

This was my chance to tell her about Grace, to squeeze a few drops of sympathy out of her. In college, Penny had taken turns dating both me and Grace, and I always thought this granted her a kind of imaginary access to our marriage and bedroom, a frightful authority to piece together both Grace's and my sexual proclivities and insecurities. But, for all of her affectations and calculated quirkiness, she had always been pathologically kind. Or at least to animals. Her basement apartment was always mobbed with stray cats, stray dogs, stray squirrels ("I don't think a non-domesticated animal can be considered a stray," I once told her; "you're not taking him in—you're kidnapping him").

There was a crosshatching of animal hair on her windshield and the coiled smell of pheromoney dog farts in the air.

"How's Pig?" I asked.

"Piglike and wonderful. Wanna pay him a visit? You've been negligent lately."

"Yes."

Her apartment was a short walk away, on sidewalks destabilized by tree roots muscling up from beneath.

...

There once was an Islander, or so I'm told, so determined to validate our Island's claim to history that he dedicated himself to uncovering archaeological proof of Sycorax, the fish-witch mother of Caliban who lived on the Island in the era before Prospero appeared. This was perhaps a generation or two before the Miranda Conference arrived on our shores. There was a problem with his theory, of course: while we believed our Island to be the inspiration for the isle of *The Tempest*, nearly everyone accepts that Shakespeare must have embellished a bit, and so while we delight at the crossover details between the play and life as we know it on the Island, we knew not to be too literalistic. This man, however, wanted proof, more proof, definitive as mortal remains, and that meant the carbon-dated bones of Sycorax. This man, this Islander, was an archeologist of some note— or at least a grave-robber of some note; no one had seen a degree from an accredited university, but they had seen the ghoulish menagerie of remains he'd uncovered, none quite witchy enough to be Sycorax.

The Island quickly became pock-marked with his dig sites, each one an open grave into which a cloud-glimpsing flaneur might stumble, each one an unsettling reminder that with the search for evidence comes the possibility of counterevidence, the specter of despair looming over all hope.

That was how the Island council put it when they ordered him to cease all digging. On the official Arolian books is this: "We, the people of the Island of Arolia, hereby file a plea that our citizen-Islanders not attempt to pin down desire with certainty, as the specter of despair looms over all hope, and an insistence on certainty undermines the very core of who we are as an Island-nation, especially when the possibility of simple and pure possibility is an option."

The man was ordered to fill in all the holes he'd dug, though he was allowed to keep the bones he'd found, the sundry femurs and such.

...

Shortly after my fourth anniversary with Grace, I stayed home one night while she went out to get a drink with a friend of hers who'd recently broken up with her boyfriend and needed Grace's shoulder to tearfully snot on. Around one in the morning, I heated chamomile tea in the microwave oven we'd received from a mercifully practical relative at our wedding. After only four years of use, that microwave was already filthy. Its inside, once a gleaming cube of white walls that looked somehow futuristic, was now splattered with the exploded guts of every meal we'd overcooked in it, so that whenever we used it now, it seemed to also be re-cooking all those tiny little morsels of food. Even if you only heated a simple mug of water for chamomile tea to help you fall asleep while your wife was out, it would come out of the microwave redolent of ambiguous leftovers, the smell acidic and clingy and sweaty and somehow always reminding me of a high school cafeteria. After one minute, the microwave beeped and in that same moment the phone rang. I tended to my tea first, taking it out of the microwave and blowing steam from its surface, before answering the phone.

It was Grace, calling from jail. She had been in a blackout when she left the bar and drove into the school's playground, so that night would always be a mystery. When they impounded her car, they found a set of golf clubs in the backseat along with a paperback copy of *The Muriel Spark Reader* and an oversized novelty clock, none of which we'd seen before. The details lay before us like clues in a locked-room riddle. I had always been a proud champion riddle-solver, but the clues in this one remained random and non sequitur, refusing to fit together into a coherent narrative.

There were fines and hours of community service and, since the jungle gym she'd crashed into was Island property, there was a mandatory stay in rehab. One month.

For the year prior to this incident, we'd been talking about having a child. I wanted a lot of kids, wanted to name them all after Thomas Kyd, from whom my dad claimed bastardly descendance ("He banged a barmaid"). I imagined a whole brood of little Thomases, Tommies, Toms.

"More toms than Neil Peart!" I told Grace.

"Is that another Rush reference?" she asked.

"Yes," I said, "sorry."

Not only did Grace express concern about my musical influences and ideas about baby names, she also expressed grave concern about all these future babies coming out of her vagina. "It's just not made for that kind of traffic," she said. While in Nueva Vista, she mentioned this to her counselor there, this American guy Chad, and Chad—all ponytail and New Age smarm—told her to try a pet first. She told this to me over the phone one night, and the next day, I got her a pet.

From the radio, I had just won a day pass to the Tempest Fest, for being the ninth caller who knew the name of James Brown's saxophonist ("Maceo! May-see-oh!"), and so I went to the Tempest Fest, with my one ticket, alone. I spent the afternoon wandering around the bb-gun firing range wedged between Caliban-wrestling contests, the

Ferris Wheel made to look like the Music of the Spheres, while eating a pretzel the size of my face, all sloppy with mustard, dodging kids with their clouds of cotton candy looming over them, until I stumbled onto the Pig Catch. Unlike all the other displays, this one hadn't even bothered with a *Tempest*-related pretense. At the Pig Catch, you did just that, tried to catch a greased pig in a rink of mud.

I wolfed down the last rib-bone curl of my pretzel and spent the next two hundred and fifty-six seconds chasing a small pig around the primordial soup. It was the most fun I'd had in a long time. While I slid headlong toward a fence-post and certain injury, the pig in front of me turned on a dime, and I managed to hook him into a headlock, breaking my momentum, and suddenly I had the pig firmly in my two-armed grip. The pig bucked and twisted and the sharp stilettos of his baby hooves dug into my chest, but I'd done it. I stood up—covered in so much mud I felt like one of the many Caliban-costumed actors roving the Fest—and delivered the pig victoriously to the proprietor of the Pig Catch, only to find that the prize was the pig itself.

When Grace emerged intact and sane from rehab at the end of the month, having steeled herself against their therapies and compulsory confessions and cultish cigarette huddles, I put our new pet pig, a small thing, maybe thirty pounds, into a box with a slender blue ribbon around his neck, and placed the box at my wife's feet, like a cat dropping the gift of a killed pigeon before its owner. We were sitting on our small balcony, celebrating her return from rehab with pizza and white zinfandel. She opened the box, but I couldn't see her expression as her hair had fallen over her down-turned face. There was a pause. Then the pig snorted. And then Grace laughed. A lot. This was hilarious, she said. She pulled the blue ribbon from the pig and let the evening wind take it up and away; the ribbon lingered there for a moment above us like aurora borealis before riding away on a current in the breeze. "I mean," Grace said, "this is a joke, right?"

No, I should have said, not a joke, wife of mine, mother of my future child, it's a gift, a symbol—we will cherish and take care of this creature, nurture it just like your Counselor Chad told us to, with his goatee and eternal state-certified wisdom; we will raise this piglet into a pig as proof that we can do it—*for real!*—hoping that whichever God we decide to raise our child and pig to believe in will see us down here being loving and responsible and show my blindly eager sperm the way to that egg in your tummy—beneath that little epicenter of skin, your perfect outie belly button, that omphalos, that center of everything, that axis mundi, with its gravitational pull to procreate—and finally join the two of us in one!

"He smells," Grace said. "Like the dumpster behind a McDonald's. I think he crapped in the box."

Ah, the sweet musk of life, my dear! Doesn't it just make your ovaries salivate?

"Where are we supposed to keep this thing?"

In our hearts, my darling.

"And what does this thing eat? Trash?"

It feeds on our love, my sweet.

"And you want me to name this thing? Are you kidding me? It's a pig!"

Yes, my love, I understand that it seems impossible to put a name to this little symbol of our love, that heart-shaped life you're holding—how can a mere sound encapsulate the beauty of it?

But all I really said was, "Do what you want with it. I'm going inside."

And so, after the discovery of the little eraser-tip under the tail determined pronouns, and after references to an unnamed "him" began to sound exalted and fearsome, he became "The Pig," then finally—like a Baby Boy named so because that was the only description of the orphan on his birth certificate—just plain Pig.

•

By the time my sperm was found to have all the alacrity of a tortoise, Grace had officially had her fill of filling Pig's food bowl, and so I took Pig to the Pet Emporium and spoke with a red-aproned clerk, explained that I wanted to give my pig away to a happy family. The clerk told me that I could post a free ad on their bulletin board for pet adoptions. I went over to the board along the side of the store and looked over the postings, all of them handwritten on official Pet Emporium index cards, got a sense of the genre's rhetoric. (*Fresh-faced little kitty!!! cute cute cute!!! NOT declawed!!!* and: *Tiger Shark! All you need is a place to keep him and he's yours!* and, simply, beautifully: *CRABS!!!*)

I picked up the pen dangling from a string, fixed to it with a creased wrap of scotch tape. I took a Pet Adoption card and wrote, *American Yorkshire Pig up for adoption*. Knowing this needed some padding, some flair, I underlined *American* and added: *He's cute, adorable, loyal and cuddly*, then added *!!!!!* When I dotted my fifth exclamation mark, I realized I had poked hard enough for a ballpoint bump to appear Braille-like on the other side of the card. I crumpled the card, tossed it, and—steeling myself to confront those damn suggestive eyebrows—called Penny. She of the Noah complex happily accepted Pig into her home.

•

Now, six years later, the backyard that Penny shared with her upstairs neighbor had gone wild with weeds, and there in the middle of it was Pig.

From that small thirty-pound piglet, Pig had grown to a sturdy hundred pounds, still pretty small for an American Yorkshire. His skin, once baby-butt pink, had become mottled and blighted with brown stains, but still managed to retain, beneath a protective layer of coarse white hair, that Band-Aid brand flesh-tone.

Pig was now sleeping in the fishnet shade of the hammock, snoring, his apnea quite suspenseful.

I knelt down, petted him. Pig lifted his lazy head and I took his ears in my hands. When I'd first held him, I had been disturbed by how human Pig's skin felt, though tougher and hairier. I got used to it over the years, but now noticed it again, the plump meniscus of his skin, webbed with creases traced dry and white, tough but alive. I sat down and rubbed Pig's ears and saw the dim afternoon light show through them, revealing a network of pink veins. Pig snorted, like a moist fart against the inside of my arm. I ran my hand over Pig's furrowed brow and scratched, the animal purring in a register low enough to vibrate my ribs where we were leaning against each other. I could feel the push and pull of Pig's lungs.

I looked up at Penny. "I want him back."

•

"A pig's skin is supposed to be the most like a human's," Grace once said. "Derik, you remember him. We hung out a lot sophomore year. I mean, dated, I guess, if nineteen-year-olds can really date. He was apprenticing, then. He's the one who gave me my butterfly. Don't look at me like that, don't get weird, you already knew that. Anyway, he needed skin to practice on, and I guess too many botched jobs had pissed off all his friends. So he'd go to butcher shops. This one in particular, Supercarne. He'd take his little toolkit up there, go in the back, plug in, and tattoo the dead pigs. Said their skin had the texture and elasticity, the responsiveness that he'd only ever felt on humans before. I remember going there to get some prosciutto once, and I actually saw one of the pigs, hanging there on a hook, completely inked, hoof to snout, just totally muddied with tats. The pig looked like a Dungeon Master's wet-dream: covered in everything from fire-breathing dragons to flying dragons to other things that only looked like dragons. Derik liked to quote Michelangelo, and I'd say, 'You mean the Ninja Turtle?' which he never got, and he'd be like, '*The Agony and the Ecstasy*, my favorite movie, how Charlton Heston says that sculpting is freeing the angel from the rock or some shit,' because he thought it was like that with tattoos, burning away your old skin, discovering something beneath. Cute idea and all, but I think he preferred working on the dead pigs. They didn't move. They were the perfect passive canvases. By the time he did my butterfly, he said the unpredictability of live skin was something he'd never get used to. Always having to anticipate how someone might move."

•

In the hotel lobby, as I walked Pig toward the elevator on a leash, the maitre d' flagged me down with a two-fingered gesture that looked more like the man was scientifically sniffing a mysterious chemical odor. When I nervously approached the reception desk, he didn't bat an eye at Pig. He said, "A delivery, sir," and pulled from behind the front desk a cardboard box the size of a microwave.

The thrill of an unexpected package! Of course, I knew the possibility that someone—Grace, a secret benefactor, Santa Claus—had sent me some wonderful, self-affirming gift would dissolve into disappointment, but for a moment it was nice to imagine. In this case, the thing delivered on its promise of disappointment by being addressed to Baxter.

I took the package, and Pig was surprisingly eager to board the elevator.

In the room, Mel and Baxter were playing video games on his computer, some sort of first-person shooter with soul-rending sound effects. They said nothing when Pig and I walked in, just leveled bovine stares at the new roommate.

"He's staying," I said.

•

Pet-tending as rehearsal for child-rearing was all wrong, I now knew.

The former teaches you to steer indomitable instincts toward something less brutish, the way those men with brooms frantically suggest the curling stone toward a straight path and calm resting, when the thing is clearly designed for destruction.

Children, on the other hand, seem benign by nature; the world has to train them to violence.

•

Months, years I tried with Grace, watching her casually micturate into a coffee mug, then, biscotti-like, dip in a thin plastic pregnancy test, and patiently watch the little window, as if it were a Polaroid slowly developing—waiting to see if a person developed in the picture—only to see the single negative blue line appear again and again.

And then: Grace's sister got pregnant. "From work," she said, as if she'd caught a cold.

Watching her give birth—actually watching it, as she'd requested Grace and I help her in the delivery room—watching, point blank, this new person crown like a groggy eyeball, then fully emerge, then, a week later, actually getting to hold him, my breath bothering the light pencil-sketched eddy of hair, the baby's marshmallow chubbiness, the eyes like security-camera lenses, and me unsure how much those eyes were taking in but afraid of what he might see, me aching for my own personal talisman of adulthood, a son.

And yet I was scared of this new person, panicked that I wasn't holding him right, that I wasn't supporting the baby's butt and head correctly and that this was messing up the feng shui of his insides and that he would die of SIDS right there in my arms. The baby just stared up at me. What did he want? Did he want me to coo baby-babble at him, the way his mother would? Did he want me to entertain him with funny faces, the way his mother would? Did he want me to produce from my shirt a lactating breast to suckle, the way his mother would?

I just held him and waited for instructions from my latent fatherly instinct—that voice of my older, wiser self, I imagined, whispering to me from some happy and successful future, telling me what to do, telling me all the things that would lead me toward that future self. With baby in hands, I waited. But I heard nothing. And while I continued to wait, the boy moved his little baby bowels, producing something with the festive look of guacamole.

•

"Is he house-broken?" Mel wanted to know.

"Doubtful," I said. I knew Penny was an advocate of something called Elimination Communication for house-training animals; though, like most theories Penny advocates, it was surely bunk.

Pig nuzzled our pile of shoes in the corner, rooted in.

"Any word from the landlady?" I asked.

"Not a one," Baxter said, sniffing the air, presumably trying to parse the animal's smell from his own.

By now, Baxter and Mel were huddled over a laptop, backs to me, screen-lit faces reflected in the window like radioactive Dickensian orphans begging for alms.

"The percentage of 'thumbs-up' votes is irrelevant," Baxter was saying to Mel, "until you factor in the total number of views and votes."

Mel produced skeptical noises.

Baxter and Mel had been decorating this place with throw pillows and various other accent accoutrements (there were harem-like silks hanging on the lampshades, casting the room in Castilian red), and I suddenly wondered how long we'd actually been here.

"Baby, don't worry about the comments," Baxter was saying. "They're just trolls, assholes looking to start a fight."

I peered over Baxter's shoulder, at the computer they were fixed to. On the screen was a website, on the website a video, in the video Baxter and Mel making bouncy love in this very room.

Mel turned to me. "You be the judge," she said. "Look at us," waving a hand at the screen. "Do you think I look bored? The comments, they say I look like I am bored, but I am not! I was feeling very orgasmic!"

Baxter said, "I think this is our best video yet, babe."

"Leonard," she said, "you be the judge."

On the screen, my tiny pixelated roommates rubbed their parts together in taut salvo. It was true, Mel did look a bit bored. I would have directed her to at least move her mouth some, moan; I would have reminded her that her inner experience of orgasm and the orgasm she communicated to the audience were two different things.

But, "I'm no judge," I said.

"Oh!" Baxter said, seeing the package I'd brought up. "Our boom mics! Trust me, babe, this'll change things."

While Baxter tore open the package, I tried to get Pig comfortable beside my bed. Mel came over to me and stuck a crumpled page under my nose. "You dropped this, from your journal."

"From my journal?"

"From your journal, you dropped it."

I read,

as someone whose constitution was built on the simple fish-centric diet of an Islander, only to move to the cream-based foods when I got older and the Island became more influenced by the Continent, I have since suffered the effects of that diet. I have found solace in discovering, in the works of the Western Canon, the wisdom of famous men on their reticent colons. This interest began for me when, during secondary school, I was perched in a stall and saw, scribbled in the grout, Flaubert's claim that "all men of letters are constipated." It was then that I considered becoming a man of letters, having already satisfied one surprising requirement. And although that has not panned out, on my one visit to the Flaubert house in Rouen, during a trip abroad, I was delighted to see a contraption Gustave's doctor-father made, a simple enematic pump rigged to a bench in a most invasive looking manner. The American Henry James has some of the most startlingly beautiful prose on this affliction in his letters to brother William. He actually had a similar backstory to me: in his youth he had a movement everyday, but when he became older all movement ceased. It was on the advice of William James that I tried the "sulfuric acid dodge," which landed me two weeks in the student infirmary. To think about this through a Freudian lens, it's interesting that while they both suffered this ailment, Flaubert, with his obsessive revising, seems more trapped in the anal retentive stage, while James, with his baggy monsters, was trapped in the anal expulsive stage. I even read in Plutarch that Alexander the Great went four years without successful passage, though that might have been a mistake of translation.

"From my journal?" I said.

"From your journal, you dropped it," Mel said.

"Oink," said the pig.

No, I thought, this was one of Grej's emails to Alli.

"Nonsense," Mel said. "That is you, that is your voice. You need more fiber."

From the corner, Baxter, holding a new microphone like a dangling phallus, said, "But I see your new buddy is getting plenty of fiber."

"Shit," I said.

"Yep," Mel said.

Baxter shouted, "House cleaning!"

•

Back in college, before Grace and I had begun dating, I spent endless hours cultivating a hoarder's aesthetic in the little black-box theater in the basement of Coyle Hall. This theater hadn't been used in years except as a storage space for props and costumes: here were the wigs from the all-male production of *The Vagina Monologues*; here were mountains of junk—coffee pots, broken clocks, opera glasses—used to stock the thrift shop in *American Buffalo*; here was the poorly constructed balcony used in that ill-fated production of *R&J* (the phrase "Romeo's concussion" was actually used in the lawsuit the boy's parents brought against the Department of Theatric Arts). And I, tired of my then-roommate's newfound dedication to Welsh clog dancing, came here to study. I'd sit comfortably on an intricately patterned chaise lounge from Norma Desmond's mansion in last year's production of the *Sunset Boulevard* musical. Swaddled in a cardigan that smelled like an attic, which I'd bought at Goodwill for two dollars because it reminded me of what Andre Gregory wore in *My Dinner with Andre*, I'd read in the quiet company of theater's leftover and disordered fragments.

This was at a point in my education when the doors of my two mentors seemed to be closed with sudden frequency.

Professor Kline's office door—cluttered with *Far Side* cartoons about Shakespeare, *New Yorker* cartoons having something to do with tenure, scotch-taped posters for lectures he'd given ten years prior—was locked, his person elsewhere, surely engaging in the behaviors that would later be detailed in official complaints. And I hadn't, of late, seen Professor Bridget Ash's emaciated figure hunched like the Grim Reaper over the department's copier, as if finally escorting that wretched machine from this earth, and her office door—so spare as to be an aesthetic statement—was likewise shut.

In that basement black-box theater I found the coziness of clutter, the permissive balm of a mess contained, both expulsive and retentive. When I moved in with Grace, however, I began—begrudgingly and bescoldingly—to learn the rightness of things in their places, began to learn the radical but eventually comforting concept of things even having places. It was training for ISNT. ISNT was a place where, if nothing else, things had places. A thing might not have anything else, but it certainly had a place.

And so, in the weeks before Grace left, I had—perhaps without realizing it—taken her seeming severity as a simple return to her old self.

·

I woke up in the hotel with one thought: Cake4Breakfast.

...

There once was an Islander, or so I'm told, a cartographer in the days when the Earth was young enough to still hold the promise of unmapped land, but old enough for the cartographer to see that promise shrinking, the specter of the unknown slowly dying. It was a paradox of his passion of which he was becoming acutely aware: the desire to discover and map, to chart certainty, driven by love not of certainty but of mystery, the necessary erasure of mystery. This young cartographer daily visited the map that Bartholomew Gosnold drew of the Island in 1602. The map was originally in the book Gosnold published upon his return to London, the manuscript held at Oxford University, but when Oxford laughed off the Island official's claims that the map should rightfully be held on the land which it depicts, one plucky Islander drew up a counterfeit and, in a daring-do feat of Arolian pride, managed to switch the two at Oxford, successfully bringing the original back to its proper home, where it now resided behind glass in our own University library. It was a remarkable document, the thin lines demonstrating a keen understanding of the vicissitudes of Atlantic shoreland, the crosshatch shadings showing a thinner thread-count for higher elevations and a more dense tangle for the lower bits of gnarled forestry. Our young cartographer couldn't check the document out of the library—indeed, it was an object of utmost security, Islanders always fearful Oxford would discover the switch and steal it back—so our protagonist took to painstakingly copying the image out in his notebook.

He used his copy to navigate a circumferencing walk around our Island, only to discover some infidelities between map and territory. As Gosnold's map had been the source for all extant maps then in use, he made note of these discrepancies and took them to Island officials. Their response was not to modify the maps but to modify the land, to bring the represented closer to the representation. Much machinery was involved.

It's never been clear which topographical details of our Island were subject to revision, something we are always keenly aware of. This slippery relationship between sign and signifier was presaged by Shakespeare when no characters in *The Tempest* seem to agree on what exactly the Island looks like, and is perhaps why—a fuck-you to the Platonic relationship between Ideal and Form—our University's Department of Theatric Arts is so strong, our suspicion that self is determined by its own representation, not the other way around.

And yet, that young cartographer, I believe, wound up walking into the ocean.

...

Alli and Grej were doing their scene work. They were sitting across from me—Grej in his casual corduroys, furrows worn smooth, and Alli in her business best—rehearsing their interview questions. I'd given them a list of the most common questions asked in status adjustment interviews, and their homework had been to write their own answers and present it to me as scene work, and presently they were on their response to the who-does-the-cooking question.

"Grej does a good bisque," Allie was saying. "It's not watery like most bisques I've had in the States." She was drinking coffee dimmed by dairy.

"Cream," Grej said. "That's the key. Alli does a spectacular Chinese thing."

"Stir fry."

"That's a bit of a rarity here, and it's just fantastic. So much soy sauce I can hear my heartbeat for days."

Cake4Breakfast, I was thinking, an American. He was, wasn't he. I was trying to call to mind his profile from that dating site. All I could summon was a blurry man beside a motorcycle. But an American, I was sure. Came here to the Island to steal away more Islanders, back to the States.

"Well?" Alli said. "How was that?"

"You've been staring at the wood knot on your desktop for quite a bit now," Grej said. "I suppose it is quite a fetching little swirl of wood." He smiled.

"It was good," I said. "Your exchanges showed wonderful

nuance. The technique of the tandem answer, finishing each other's sentences and whatnot, nicely creates a sense of you two being one unit. Like Romeo and Juliet finishing each other's metric lines."

"That was Alli's idea."

I realized I was staring at the wood knot again, wondering at a flaw that can make a solid turn liquid, stability slip and swirl. In that profile, Cake4Breakfast had said he was a good listener.

"But," I said. "That's just not gonna fly here."

Alli and Grej adjusted their postures, formalized their spines a bit.

"I mean, who actually listens to each other?" I said. "You know?"

"I don't understand," Alli said.

"Let's return to some acting one-oh-one here."

Alli crossed her arms, cocked her head. "Okay."

"Motivation. Everyone has an agenda. You must enter every scene *wanting* something from your scene partner. Yes?"

"And we want to pass the interview," Grej said.

I said, "Am I your scene partner? Who's your partner here?"

Alli pulled her lips between her teeth and examined the ceiling panels, while eager Grej's eyes were churning slot-machine reels of indecision.

"You're each other's scene partners," I said. "What do you want from *each other*?"

Grej turned to Alli, who was performing impatience beside him.

"You don't have to tell me," I said. "You don't have to tell each other. In fact, best not to."

"We don't keep secrets from each other," Grej said.

"That's adorable, but you do on my stage." I was standing up now, unsure how that had happened. "On my stage, you want something from your partner, you truly *need* something from them, something that can't, for the dramatic sake of the scene, be directly articulated. And that's the glue, isn't it, the tension between knowing and telling. But you can tell me, as an extra-scene entity, you can tell me what that is."

I said some other things, and I recall at this point Alli asking me to calm down.

"Besides," I said, sitting down, "what kind of man advocates for the eating of cake for breakfast?"

"Excuse me?" Alli said.

"What?" I said.

"I don't believe either of us mentioned cake for breakfast," Grej said.

"You know him?" I said. "Tell me."

"Know who?" one of them said.

"Cake4Breakfast," I said.

"Seems a little late for breakfast," Grej said.

"And too early for cake," Alli said.

I looked for that wood knot, was suddenly unsure where in my desktop it had been. I crossed my legs. I folded my hands over my knee.

"Let's try the scene again. This time, break the script. Interrupt. Contradict. Live."

There was a white-noised moment of resettling, a tacit agreement to reset.

"Another thing," I said. "Keep your hands out of sight. That's a rule."

•

The hands, they can signal in ways you never considered, my predecessor had explained to me. The hands are themselves signals, the farthest reaching physical agents of the body. This was why interviewees, when interviewed together, must keep their hands below the table, on their laps, out of sight: interviewees were not supposed to be able to communicate silently with each other in ways not comprehended by the interviewer.

Consider The Addams Family, my predecessor had said: that character Thing, the nuance and range of expression in a performance limited to five fingers. He raised his hand—which didn't seem to have the expressive range of Thing Addams, clawed as it was by arthritis—and pointed towards his own temples. "You're starting to lose a bit up there."

There was a unique kind of horror at having an almost dementia'd man identify you as a fellow loon, accusing you of losing your mind. This was the confirmation I'd feared my whole life. But no. As my predecessor continued tapping his own head, I realized he was accusing me of starting to lose my hair, not my mind.

"Do what I did," my predecessor said. "The plugs are a miracle."

My predecessor's hair gave mixed signals. It had receded uniformly as if to make room for something impressive to be staged on the man's impeccable pate. But there remained the pointillism of abandoned hair plugs, a single row of them, like a picket fence along the top border of his forehead.

"I'll consider it," I said, thinking, *I hope I go gently into that good night.*

My predecessor raised his hand into the air between us, as if for inspection. He came back to his main point—"Be careful of hands"—and returned his eyes to their normal resting spot, just to the left, on my earlobe. I wondered if forsaking eye-to-eye contact for eye-to-ear contact was a strategy, as it did seem like a brilliantly infuriating way to create unsettling and unspecified discord when interviewing. But I wasn't an interviewee. I put my hands on the desk.

Since retirement, my predecessor had spent his days swimming through a finally-confirmed dementia, offering me, when I visited, a kind of connect-the-dots, fragments of language, of life, his past finally more present than the present. I think he was happy.

•

I gave Alli and Grej fifteen minutes to rehearse their scene in the parking lot, and I could now see them through the window. Watching two people rehearse while still on book was like watching babies parallel play; any appearance of interaction was accidental.

The fact that everyone wanted to leave the Island, to head to the States, was nothing more than an elaborate confirmation process, confirming that yes you are a person living in a place. Everyone left. Had Grace already hopped a flight with Cake4Breakfast? Was she already American?

•

The traffic from the Tempest Fest's initial spasm of excitement had dissipated, but the streets were still strewn with oversized novelty foam hands with index fingers extended, cans of budget beer crushed on the ground.

I hadn't retrieved my car since abandoning it in the traffic jam, and now I was finally walking Pig back to where I'd left it. I fully expected to find the car flipped on its side with graffiti across its undercarriage. But when Pig and I got to the car, there was no graffiti and it was still standing on all four Goodyears. Ignored by catastrophe, passed over: the fire and Grace's abandonment, surely, having marked my car with the lamb's blood of heartbreak, filled my quota of hardship for the year, or at least for the week. (Or the month? How long ago did Grace leave?)

I hustled Pig into the back seat, then rustled the rusty engine awake, drove off. The citrusy tang of shampoo was still redolent in my hair. The Madrid's low-flow showerhead had all the hydraulic force of a nonagenarian at a urinal, and the hot water didn't last long enough for me to wash all the Pert Plus from my scalp. My skin still felt astringent from the hotel soap.

It was Saturday.

Pig in the back, his snout leaving the snail-trails of snot on the window, I drove to Alli and Grej's apartment. The address had come up in their emails, from when they found the place, and I just wanted to get a sense of things.

•

It was in the southwest, which we referred to as Sou'est.

I had last been to that little nub of the Island with Grace on antiquing trips. There was something odd about that area, sparsely inhabited by that notably American phenomenon: antique shops. Where I came from, the northeastern ridge of the Island, there were antique stores and there were thrift shops, and never the twain shall meet. An antique store was an austere Faberge egg of a place, a museum of things not to touch, costly breakables that could disintegrate from the corrosive oils on your grabby hands. And a thrift shop was a junk shop, operated by hoarders with the smallest sense of the entrepreneurial. Sou'est was the Mecca of junk.

When Grace and I, in our antique crawl, rummaged through the asthmatic storefronts of Sou'est, back in the upswing of marriage, when we were still gathering things as if for an endless dinner party (because we never knew when we might need a sterling silver serving platter, we just never knew), before it entered the downswing, the stage of hauls to all those thrift shops (because, really, when were we ever going to need *this*?), I stood in a cluttered nook, the air made palpable by dust motes that illustrated for the eye the laws and principles of aerodynamics as you moved through the atmosphere. Amid a disturbing and unironic collection of Sambo figurines from the American South, I found and puzzled over a single fraying friendship bracelet. I troubled the unbraiding purple and green, looking for bulbous inconsistencies in the dense and uniform ladder of knots, anything that might betray it as handmade, by nubby undexterous fingers at a summer camp, not just some vending machine trinket but something that had once tied the affections of two people. If there was, however, a real person behind this flimsy rat's tail of fabric, she'd been too bent on perfection to reveal herself here.

·

Turns out, those 'tique stores created a kind of wagon-circle of a neighborhood, at the center of which was a single apartment complex. What at first looked to be barnacles on a road sign turned out to be gunshot divots from a population bored to the point of property violence. The weeds reaching up through the sign's hollow post sprouted into a mohawk of blonde grass.

The apartment building featured a fascistic blend of blocky imposition and either neoclassical or homoerotic flair: in short, a Lego-y thing with a pissing-faun fountain out front. The cars snaggled into spots had the hand-me-down look of German engineering thickly dusted with disinterest. Appeals for ablution fingered onto windows had themselves dirtied over.

I pulled to the pebbly shoulder across the street. My steering wheel left flecks of plastic in the sweaty creases of my palms, and the car's floor mats showed where I'd heeled through, but I could still consider the car new: its contours still accorded to the current fashion of car shapes. That seemed sufficient to be above suspicion. But, just to be sure, I pulled out my cell phone, feigned a conversation. Without realizing it, this imaginary conversation was with Grace, details of dinner ingredients discussed.

Apartment number seven was surely on the first floor. That corner on the right, maybe. Alli had said something about watching Grej leave for work in the morning, a view of the parking lot.

Pig made a sinusy gurgle, gave a deflating fart and crumpled to the seat.

I cracked the window an inch, then got out. I listened to the tinkling of the car's engine cooling, made a scrotal adjustment, then walked across the street. The building's parking lot was at one time concrete, a concrete that had since cracked, ceded to the tumescent roots below. I tried to recall the make and model of their car, recalled only that it was an old thing they shared (Alli's version), or an old thing Grej bought and shared with her (Grej's version).

I walked closer to the apartment building's front door, looked over the square panels of slatted mailboxes, the surnames of tenants printed on masking tape. The name for apartment number seven, however, was illegible, the tape having peeled in the weather, bled its ink into illegibility. This surely meant its residents had lived here long enough,

but Alli and Grej claimed to have moved in only five months
ago.

•

When I returned to the car, there was a neat ziggurat
of poo on the backseat, the culprit sitting in the front, his
hooves folded daintily beneath him.

At the self-service car wash, I pulled into a stall, opened
both back doors. Into the small metal box mounted on the
wall, I fed some quarters; after a lifetime of laundromats, it
was impossible to use just one quarter for anything other
than my weekly wash without experiencing a serrated pang
of guilt, thinking of all those socks I'd have to hang-dry in
the bathroom, but this was a necessary expense. I picked
up the hose, which had enough water pressure to not so
much wash away as obliterate Pig's ordure, and Pig himself
whimpered in the front seat, ducked below the glovebox
for cover.

When I was finishing up, my cell phone rang. On the
display, the caller ID said *Baxter.*

I answered and Baxter said, "Are you coming back
tonight?"

"Yeah."

"Can you pick up some celery?"

"Celery?"

"Mel is making chicken stock. With the leftover carcass
from lunch."

"I suppose."

"She says a bay leaf too."

Nearby, the birch trees were shedding bark like pencil shavings. The whole Island was about to start shedding. Fall was coming, and this place had a lot of leaves to drop. The year before, I'd had to use a snow shovel to scoop rain-sludged leaves from the storm drain, the leaves having already turned into a kind of papier-mâché.

•

In order to get back to the Madrid, I had to drive past the University, through that neighborhood where every establishment's walls were flared with bumper stickers, band fliers, nonsensical broadsides, along with homemade adverts for piano lessons, crochet lessons, ballroom dance lessons, the bottom of each a British smile of tabs with phone numbers; the bars that had a don't-ask-don't-tell policy regarding age and offered food that comfortingly reminded clientele of not-so-long-ago junior high cafeterias; the coffee shops that attempted to blur the line between baristas and eighteenth-century alchemists; the pizza parlors that offered creative toppings and had punningly named their pies after famous characters from literature, so all the lettered youths could nosh slices of Ancient Marinara with Albatross (barbequed chicken) and nod knowingly. On the sidewalk, a family—preening Mom, dutiful Dad, clad in University colors that vibrated queasily on the retina—took pictures of their soon-to-be freshman, his face flecked and shined by adolescence, arms and torso tending toward a simian proportionality, posing before a bronze statue of a Prospero whose face was bukkaked with birdshit.

At the grocery store I found the celery, grabbed a crunchy bunch of stalks. Undergrads, girls still in stilettos, drank Gatorades in aisle eight, commented on last night's happenings. I walked by, just to see if I could still be seen.

•

At the Madrid, Mel and Baxter cooked in tandem. She hovered over the hotplate, prodding a potted something with a spoon. The hotplate was a new addition to the room, snatched off the side of the road in the ruins of a student district. Baxter played sous chef, shucked shellfish in the bathroom tub. The room was humid as a hamam. You couldn't open the windows, Baxter pointed out. They'd been nailed shut: too many jumpers. The bodega below sued when it got tired of replacing its awning.

We ate at a card table propped between the beds, Mel and Baxter sitting on theirs, me on mine.

Mel looked at me. "So?" she said, chewing something stubborn, cartilagey. "Where do you go when you go out?"

"Mel," Baxter said. "That's none of our —"

"I'm just asking. These are not normal working hours. It makes me feel very unsettled, having this in-and-out all the time."

Yes—although Baxter and Mel themselves kept remarkably strange hours. The only job between the two of them I'd been able to identify was Baxter's bafflingly scheduled gig at Madame Tussaud's Wax ("They don't want to call it a *museum*," Baxter explained with the quiet pride of an industry insider. "I clean the figures, the dust, what have you, and wash their hair. You can touch 'em, you know, do anything you want.")

Mel now said to me, "We've worked hard to make a home here, to feel settled."

I arranged the withered greens in my bowl, stirred the oil-spotted broth puddle below.

"It's okay," Baxter said to me. "You don't have to answer. She's just concerned about you, is all. We've both been concerned, Mel and I."

I was beginning to realize I had a talent for finding needs in people, filling them like caulk in cracks.

•

That night in bed, I scrolled through my phone, rediscovered a series of stills I'd taken with Grace. This must have been the last costumed series we did before the Department of Theatric Arts finally changed the locks on the storage warehouse, meaning the keys Grace had kept since graduation no longer granted us late-night access to the cache of costumes: Cleopatra's diadem, Annie's pinafore, Eliza Doolittle's parasol. This series of photos, our last sitting, featured me (in ruff-collar and puff-and-slash sleeves) as Richard of Gloucester, and Grace (in kirtle, girdle, and partlet) as Queen Anne. We'd performed for ourselves act one, scene two: after admitting to the grieving

Anne that he's killed her husband, Tricky Dick effectively seduces her. "The finest piece of cocksmanship in Western literature," Grace had said. "She's Silly Putty in his gimpy hands." Our performance was only a pantomime for the camera—just a thing we did—but I still felt the huge gulf Grace's superlative had opened up, unsure I could fill it. When the photo-series continued into the imagined consummation, I noticed the foreshortening effect the pantaloons had on my pecker.

"Turn off your phone," Mel said from the neighboring bed. "No screens this late. Blue light interferes with your sleep."

I did as she said. I got out of bed, fished the charger from my bag and plugged in my phone, out of reach from the bed. But when I did, I found in my bag the creased page of a printed email: *And I am imagining him exhaling that smoke, watching it float up lighter than air and then into her lungs, the ineffable made tangible, something that can stain, that lingered long after their lives diverged, in 1592.* In bed, I reread, in the red glow of the digital clock, this last sentence, and I wondered about the choice of "stain." It could have been variously translated as "mark," like a target, or "smudge," like something becoming illegible.

•

In the morning, I stepped into the shower and cut the soles of my feet: shards of crab exoskeleton scattered in the basin.

I went about my day; I delicately walked its periphery.

There was a new adjustment of status interview to prepare for—finally someone moving to the Island. And yet the file revealed a couplehood of little consequence.

I called home just to hear the ring veer eventually into voicemail.

I had the run of myself.

...

There once was an Islander, or so I'm told, so taken with the Aeolian Harp formation on the Island's northern headlands that he became determined to prove it wasn't just the geology of the Island that had distorted itself toward music, but the flora and fauna as well. He supposedly had this revelation while standing on the corner of Ferdinand Avenue and Hatbrim Road, above which was strung four telephone wires, and on which wires sat a cluster of birds, silhouetted into black whole notes. He returned to that very corner the next day, having pushed, on a dolly whose wheels couldn't stay true, his mini grand. He sat at the piano, there on the sidewalk, and plunked out each note the birds formed for him. The man and his piano and his bird-borne arias became an attraction in part because of the ephemeral nature of the music. A string of notes would only repeat as long as the birds on the wires stayed still, which was never that long. You'd stand at the intersection and catch a simple three-bird melody that pulled at something lonesome in your sternum, and then: a gust of wind, the birds would rearrange, and it would suddenly turn jaunty and plucky, never to return.

Soon, someone decided this ephemerality just couldn't stand, that everything beautiful must be wrestled to the page. This new man sat beside the piano player, studiously transcribed. The piano player did not seem to notice or care. When this note-taker began publishing the sheet music, more Islanders showed up to the corner of Ferdinand and

Hatbrim, making requests. Each song, as published, was named for the date and time it was played, and so these requests took the form of people simply saying dates long past. "June eleventh, five-thirteen a.m." Or: "February sixth, ten-forty-six a.m." The piano player, unfazed— "September twenty-ninth, eleven thirty-five"—kept playing in the present. According to multiple accounts, however, the birds themselves began taking the requests—"August ninth, four-thirteen, p.m."—moving themselves into the past arrangements the listeners so loved. The piano player had no choice but to return to these old tunes. Eventually, the birds who landed on the wires formed only the old hits, refused to find new patterns, new arrangements. Today, the piano player is gone, the wires and birds too. Instead, speakers mounted nearby play tinny recordings of those old bird tunes.

...

That evening, I was on my way out the door, passing Patricia's desk, when I heard, "Some big things coming this way, Mr. Nist."

After I confirmed that I had not voided myself from fright, I turned to see Mr. Y. sitting at Patricia's desk.

"Evening," I said, my jangled nerves giving the word an extra syllable or two.

Mr. Y. held up what looked to be a piece of trash, a crumpled paper something. "Do you know what season it is?"

I thought for a moment. I didn't actually know.

"Tempest Fest," he said. "And do you know what the headliner is?"

"A production of *The Tempest*?"

Mr. Y. stood up. He walked over to me and held up the crumpled piece of paper. "By an American company." He shoved the paper in my hand. "From New York."

I looked down at the paper, unfolded it.

"Leonard, this could be big. American interest in the Island. Presaging a new influx of peoples."

The flyer in my hand certainly had the words *The Tempest* on it, though the iconography was more incarceral than insular.

Before he could listen to my qualms with this, Mr. Y. was grabbing his coat from the hanger, flaring it around his shoulders like a bullfighter with his cape, and rushing out the door to the Tempest Fest.

I failed to share his excitement. The evidence that he'd shoved into my now-paper-cut hands was not proof of a renaissance of interest in our home; it was proof that, post Miranda Conference, American theater producers had moved so far beyond the real-life inspiration for Prospero's Island that they now felt entirely free to restage the play with non-Island settings, like, in this case, Sing-Sing. And yes, I get it. I spent the best of my youth radicalizing otherwise staid productions of the classics, but those were classics whose etiology wasn't the foundation of my country's identity. Professors Kline and Ash always claimed that these interventionist stagings were acts of interrogation into the assumptions on which the original was built, and, sitting in my car in the parking lot, looking over the flyer for the play—its warden-like Prospero and prison-striped Caliban, all striated by the shadows of prison bars—I certainly felt interrogated, the panicked pang of defense: a need to justify our true history, barbed by anger.

•

Pig was in the back seat, had spent my workday there, but now my hasty and angrily swerving drive down to Tempest Fest woke him. He made a sound like a rusty door in a horror movie slowly creaking open.

The Tempest Fest had taken over most of Gosnold Square, events and vendors and sundry thematically related shenanigans spilling out as if from a toy chest.

I parked beside a man who'd repurposed a Chewbacca

costume for some Caliban cosplay and was presently pissing forcefully against a fire hydrant.

I walked the few blocks into the fray. Here was the Storm Simulator for act one, scene one, Boatswain barking for ticket-buyers out front. Here was the Ariel-Lift, wherein an attendee could be strapped with bungee cords to "fly" around spirit-like, most takers, already drunk on sack-wine, hopefully holding their puke until they were safely grounded. I'd seen these attractions many times, their signs flecking off paint. Here was a new one: an arcade of shooter games revised, guns replaced with magical Prospero staffs. I made my way to the act-four Masque: a buffet-style arrangement of foods and sack, Greco-styled go-go dancers about. I calmed myself on pulls of sack, the slippage of sweaty pasties.

Fortified by fortified wine, I marched toward the marquee blaring the name of our play. I knew this must have been the American production because they'd opted for the oversize letters. I didn't have too much of a plan, but the sack in my system was lending some confidence to my indignation, so I figured I'd take advantage of that and go shout some stuff at the American invaders, their pilfering of our play, our history.

People were clotting the place, bodies describing spirals around me. The choreography of drunken crowds always seemed one of narrowly missed collisions.

Between me and the theater was the 4-D diorama, which, every year, was constructed in the middle of Gosnold Square as an immersive and interactive *Tempest* experience, attendees progressing through the play as if through a haunted house, temporal space and physical space becoming one. Ever since I was a kid, this had been my favorite.

I got in line. *Tempest*-based tourism while en route to indignant protest in no way delegitimized said protest. I bought a ticket.

With a group of other ticket-clutchers, I walked into the first room, darkened but for the seepage of light from the door closing behind us, and I noticed the floor: large black trash bags cut into overlapping panels, duct-taped together into a crinkling carpet, water already beading and running together in rivulets, beading and rivulleting again, dots and lines, the water doing its own morse-code dance of panic, as the storm was coming. Then: concussions of light and air-borne mist like needles on the skin, actors suddenly in front of us, slickered Boatswain shouting at royals Antonio and Alonso. The effects of light and rain were too much for my slightly crapulent equilibrium, so I hurried to the next room, the next scene: a Styrofoam cliff overlooking a painting of the post-storm sea; Prospero, in a white beard peeling at the sideburns, spirit gum gleaming on the actor's stubble, giving the lowdown to Miranda—played by Dr. Philomena, our Island's spunky pharmacist— explaining to her that there's no need to feel empathy for the victims of the storm, as it wasn't a real storm, just a cook-up of his own concoction: a curious emploration, I always thought, Prospero the illusionist, Prospero the cold-hearted pragmatist, denier of illusion, the god who mocks belief, now giving his daughter his history, their history, her history, *who am I*, and how he's hijacked his usurper-brother, his plans to hatch some revenge.

Some of the other audience members stunk like wet dogs from the previous scene, and I let myself through the velour curtains, progressed to Caliban's entrance. In this room, the first thing I noticed—something I hadn't for some reason noticed in previous years—was that we had, of course, a new set of actors playing Prospero and Miranda. A curious side-effect of conflating the spatial and temporal experience of the narrative was this multiple casting, fragmenting personhood, each moment isolated from the rest creating an imperceptibly differentiated identity, the number of selves that one has, or really that one *is*, entirely dependent on the unit of measurement used to apprehend time, Schrodinger's Caliban.

Besides, I liked these actors better. While Caliban was writhing in the corner, explaining gruntingly the role he'd been trapped in by Prospero—his language and *ipso facto* identity given to him by the magician himself—I noticed a man standing oddly close to the scene, his mime-in-the-wind posture looking familiar, the rat-tail of hair. It was Grej. I moved toward him, through the turnstile elbows of fellow audience members, saw his face clearer in the blue-green gels of the hanging stage-lights, his face turned three-quarters away. Finding myself now within earshot, now within arm's swat, I was about to say something, when he turned away, exited to the next scene. There were two scenes one could exit into: this was where you, as an audience member, had to decide from whose perspective you were compelled to understand the story, from that of all-powerful magician and exiled Duke Prospero, who longed for revenge and to return to his Dukedom, or that of Caliban, Island native and slave of Prospero. In past years, I'd always—of course—chosen the Prospero door. But now Grej went through the Caliban door. I followed.

At a safe distance, I followed Grej through room after room, scene after scene, as Caliban got shit-hammered with Trinculo and Stephano; followed him as Caliban dubbed the drunkards his new masters and plotted to drive a nail through Prospero's head; followed him as the three steal Prospero's clothes and are hunted by Prospero's hellhounds; followed him finally into the last scene where Caliban is forgiven for his insubordination. This scene Grej did not stick around for. He made a quick dash for the final curtain and was gone. I followed, wondering what I would say when I caught up to him, wanting, ultimately, just a simple confirmation that things could be simple, the movements and vagaries of love easy to predict. But when I exited the final curtain and was back outside, he was gone. He had disappeared into the crowd of sack-drunk Fest-attendees. There, before me, was the American interventionist production that I'd come to protest, but I didn't have it in me anymore.

I was tired and blood-heavy from the wine.

Back in the car, Pig eyed me in a way I liked to imagine was sympathetic but I suddenly realized, as the animal began to gnaw on the soaked seat, was a simple expression

of hunger. I'd been expecting him to subsist entirely on my
takeout leftovers.

I remembered how Penny's place was stocked like a
bomb shelter with cans of pet food.

•

I drove to Penny's, pulled up and saw her outside,
watering the wisteria that, draped like feather boas around
her yard, gave her house the look of a burlesque dressing
room. Not that the Island had those sort of establishments.
They were still on the outlawed list from centuries past,
along with anal sex and public donkey trading.

As I approached, Penny pointed the hose to the sidewalk.
"Hey!" she said. "Why didn't you tell me about you and
Grace?"

"Can I get some food for Pig? I'm not even sure what his
diet is."

"I talked to her on the phone this morning." She pointed
at me with the semi-flaccid hose, its weak stream of water
splashing my feet.

"Please. Pig is really hungry."

"Why didn't you tell me? What's wrong with you?" She
seemed wobbly. In her other hand, she held a coffee mug
sporting a cocktail parasol.

"Where's Grace? Did she say?"

"Pig's on a high potassium diet. It's for his kidneys. I
have some special canned stuff you can have. But I have to
special order it and they're like seven-fifty a can, so."

"Is Grace on the Island? Have the police questioned her about the fire? I'm pretty sure the police are going to be questioning her about the fire. Tell her the police are going to be questioning her about the fire."

"Why didn't you just tell me? You know I did my grief therapy certification. I know it's not the same, but it probably is. I'm so close to finishing my certification."

"Can I just have the food, please?"

•

She let me inside, and I braced for the assault of the animals—recalling being mauled by the feral menagerie she kept—but her place was now free of fauna, save for the assortment of thrift-shop stuffed animals she'd bought for her various creatures to play with, masticate, decapitate. Those horrifying things were still scattered everywhere, their lifeless bodies bearing fresh cottony wounds.

Her duplex was full of bean bag furniture, and, not noticing the footprint-puddles I left on her hardwood, she plopped down into one such sack and sipped her bloody mary, identifiable by the tomato-juice-mustache it gave her. "The food's in the pantry."

"So?" I said. "Where did all your furry woodland creatures go?"

She sighed, let her head fall back on the beanbag chair. "My neighbor reported me." Then, in English, she said: "That cunt."

When Penny got crapulous, she got pirate-mouthed (her

expression). After a semester in London, she'd come back with a new liberal appreciation for their c-word, though now it only came out in moments like this.

She continued in English: "You saved Pig just in time. The pigs—I mean, not real pigs like Pig, but the pigs as in the fuzz, the heat, the coppers—they showed up this morning and took away my babies, spouting animal cruelty laws." She added a juicy belch.

Most of what I knew about physiology I'd learned from movies. If someone gets knocked out in a brawl, a simple splash of water will rouse them. If someone gets shit-hammered, a cup of coffee will right her. I put some water on, while Penny curled herself up like a cinnamon roll. I pulled Penny's newest coffee-making contraption from the sink, still boggy with that morning's grounds. I rinsed it out and started preparing a fresh cup, only guessing at the specifics of its operation.

"They wouldn't even let me keep D'Artagnan," she said.

I remembered D'Artagnan, the French Mastiff she'd found sniffing around the upturned rowboats on the shore. Grace and I had once dog-sat D'Artagnan, and when we had sex—that is, Grace and I—we had to lock him in the other room because he thought I was attacking Grace and would try to maul me. He'd probably been raised in a junkyard, weaned on the sinewy shanks of whatever hobos he could kill, and he had a habit of pawing at your nuts like a prizefighter on a speed bag.

"I'm sorry to hear that," I said, surprising myself with sincerity.

When the coffee was ready, I poured it into a mug that had a picture of someone's ugly dog digitized onto it. This dog, however, was not one of Penny's charity cases; she'd never met this mutt. She'd found the mug at a thrift shop for fifty cents. She prized people's kitchy personalized possessions, her apartment filled with all these items inscribed, in one way or another, to others. Or at least that had been my diagnosis of her back in college. College: those four small years of confused clarity that I should stop trying to drag kickingly into my thirties. Now, standing in Penny's living room, I realized I was wearing my college sweatshirt, that signifier of my knowledge of signifiers, now as worn as a coffee-shop copy of *Candide*.

"Thank you, my darling," Penny said, accepting the coffee. She paused to admire the dog on the mug, his downturned eyes and unnervingly humanoid set of teeth making him look—she always insisted—like Jean-Paul Belmondo. She said, "I thought I saw him the other day. I swear, someone was walking this dog down by the park, so I shouted, 'Jean-Paul Sartre!' But he didn't look. Must not have been him."

"Jean-Paul Sartre? What happened to Jean-Paul Belmondo?"

She glared at me. "Belmondo? The mug mutt has always been Jean-Paul Sartre. Don't you remember anything? I've always said he looks existential."

"No, no," I said. "You found that mug after seeing *Breathless*. That's what you always said. And you said he looked like Jean-Paul Belmondo. And he does. Look at those teeth! They're practically veneers!"

"You've always been the jealous kind. Jean-Paul Belmondo is a beautiful man. He was never, nor will he ever be, likened to a mongrel cur, cute though that cur may be." She ran her eyes over the mug.

"Where is Grace?" I said. "Is she still on the Island? Is she with Cake4Breakfast?"

"I can't tell you," she said, sipping. "That is something I most definitely cannot tell you." A spot of coffee had appeared on her pants and she worried it with her thumb, blurring the dull brown into the denim. "D'Artagnan slept here," she said. She poked the beanbag chair.

I helped her to her feet and led her into the bedroom. I cleared the plush rabbits and bears from her bed. (Penny slept with stuffed animals like, as she once quipped, "a taxidermist who takes her work home with her," then she beat-boxed a rimshot.) She flopped down onto the bed.

"Leonard," she said.

"Grace," I said.

"Penny," Penny said.

"Huh?"

"When are you gonna leave?"

"I've got plans," I said, sitting on what I thought was another bean bag chair but what turned out to be a pile of laundry. "Once I save up a bit more. You know, New York's expensive. Soon, though, soon."

Her face muffled by a pillow, she said, "I meant leave my house. I want to sleep, and it's not a spectator thing."

"Oh, right," I said, fighting my way out of the laundry pile.

"But of course you thought I meant leave the Island," she said. "Can't blame Grace. No one likes being treated like a holding pattern."

Once I got my footing, I repeated her quip about her sleep not being "a spectator thing," and I chuckled. "Didn't you do that theater piece where you slept on stage in front of the audience?"

She propped her head up. "That was a sleep study. Because of my apnea. Not everything is a theater piece, dipshit."

Back in my car, I said to Pig, "Forgot to get the food."

•

It was Baxter who broke the news. When I entered the hotel room, before I could even unleash Pig, he said: "Results in on the fire."

"Arson," I said.

"Accident."

"What?"

Pig bucked against the leash, and as I untethered him, Baxter explained: "The landlady was retrofitting for storm protection. Had to rewire the whole place so in the event of a big one, the place was outfitted with generators. I guess some of that wiring was maybe a bit rusty, got a bit itchy behind the stucco. Apparently the whole thing spread undetected in the wiring, hidden in the walls. By the time it flared out of electrical sockets on every floor, there was nothing to do but shit your pants and run. I know that's what I did."

"No," I said. "That's not right." Pig bucked again, and I realized I still hadn't unleashed him, had only made teasing overtures toward unbuckling him. I tried again. "That's simply not right," I said, my thumb getting snagged in the buckle's clamp.

"I know, they said lightning," Baxter said. "Turns out the witness across the street who reported the lightning has a neurological problem that causes him to see flashes."

"It was Grace, had to have been."

"The grace of fire," Baxter said. "That's pretty, but I can only tell you what the guy on the phone said. Apparently it's a good thing, too, that we got outta that place with its faulty storm fitting, because there's a big one coming. The woman on the news said."

A pang of discord in my solar plexus made me pace. So much had I balanced on the symmetry of those two fires bookending my relationship with Grace that all now seemed epistemologically fraught.

•

Later, in the office, I went looking through the transcripts of old adjustment of status interviews I'd conducted. Printouts, formatted like playscripts, now yellowing with age, annotated in my jittery hand to point out consistencies—of facts but also of a basic ethos—to gauge what in official ISNT communique we are to call legitimacy but what I began to think of as basic character.

I was wondering about how Alli and Grej might appear

in the marginalia-decorated transcripts of my American counterpart, imagined the lines of red connecting the tonal harmonies across answers, like the contour lines of a fully formed, fleshy person there on the page, contained and packaged, complete.

•

"That's your failing," Grace once said to me, one undergraduate night, the humidity malarial, the mosquitoes peckish. "You're a tyrant of meaning."

She was referring, ostensibly, to a play I was directing, a student-penned play of ever-branching narratives that never resolved, into which I was trying to place certain millinerial echoes, offering the audience stability in headwear, having just discovered the school's stash of old-timey derbies and trilbies. Back then, her swift diagnoses of me were exhilarating, that sudden sense of being stripped naked, the sharp stiletto of judgment on my chest. A minute after she said this we were scrambling through a hasty fuck.

We'd tried, just the once, to invite real pain—i.e., physical pain, and my conflation of *real* and *physical* did not escape Grace's attention—into the bedroom. This, after years of jokes about studded leather, years of pantomiming whip cracks, years of posing each other in sex scenes we'd imagined into the S&M-tinged relationships of *The Lion in Winter* and *Who's Afraid of Virginia Woolf*; years of costuming ourselves for stagings of scenes from *The Tropic of Cancer*, cheating out for Grace's digital camera, a gift from her father. We finally—in a moment of sexual boredom, or liberation, or both simultaneously disguising themselves as the other—spent a Thursday night shopping for a sex paddle in the red light district of the Internet (CUSTOMERS WHO BOUGHT THE SALOME SWATTER, we were informed, ALSO BOUGHT THESE ITEMS), ultimately settling on the blue plastic one with the holes in it. (Me: "Why's it got holes?" Grace: "Less air resistance, obviously.") We even paid for the express shipping from the States, and the thing arrived on Saturday, bubble-wrapped with a sender sticker so vague the mailman must have known it was something salacious, and as we unwrapped it, I nervously popped some of the bubble wrapping, and pretty soon Grace wound up and whacked me on my bare butt, and I let out a sound like a dog's squeaky toy. All energy quickly drained from my pecker and flooded my tear ducts. "Baby, baby," Grace said, now cradling me, there on the floor beside our bed, head to breast, stroking my temple, "there, there, it's okay." But I couldn't stop, couldn't stop crying. It just kept going, increasing in intensity, something I couldn't catch up with, a runaway thing, brakes failing on a steep street, but I didn't want it to stop—this, this whatever she was doing, being a new contour of my wife that I was suddenly compelled to trace, find the depth of instinct.

She didn't want kids. She'd made that clear by now, said she could handle only one child in her life.

Eventually she stood up to get a box of tissues from the bathroom, for me to blow my nose, breathe again, and when she wasn't in the room, my sobs stopped, but resumed, uncontrollably, when she came back, carrying that hibiscus-decorated box.

•

There was more to it, of course; more to most of it, less to the rest. The details that had once meant so much, that had served as easy referents—the lunar pocks of acne scars, for example, slung over her shoulder and concealed in the mottled wings of a tattoo butterfly: a simple symbol of intimacy, as only I knew to search for them there—those now seemed slippery, eliding clear meaning, the butterfly refusing to stay still long enough for me to pin its wings in the shadow box.

I often asked interviewees about their partners' tattoos, if applicable. Those doodles to mark identity often bifurcate that identity into competing versions, his and hers, like wedding-registry towels. A Chinese character on a bicep, like a gnarled and thorned pound sign: to him a symbol of strength, to her a symbol of dubious decision-making. But they, these couples, they make their peace with these discrepancies; indeed, discrepancy often seems architecturally essential to their peace, like tension on a keystone.

The thick black contours of Grace's monarch had started to go blurry those past few years, but there was still the slight embossment on the skin, those lines raised swollen, faintly, as if angry. She threatened more. "Once you get one," she said, and I could hear the ellipsis in her held breath. I imagined the accumulated cluttering, my wife disappearing beneath an inky palimpsest, all those illegible symbols.

Instead, she disappeared into an ersatz Jill.

"The funny thing about contour lines," she said, one sultry Sunday—sultry simply because she'd called it sultry, effectively making it so—"is that they're an artist's conceit." She was on her belly, her head flopping off the edge of the bed, while I traced the puckered-mouth outline of her back butterfly. "We don't really have borders."

At the time, I felt included in that word, *we*, cozily snugged into the syllable along with her: no borders, not between us. But fitting *into* something requires borders around that something, ensuring exclusivity, and the word itself lacked the contour lines of hard consonants, was only air, propulsive breath. And, while it might retain a Frenchly hint of assent, the word *we* always sounded like it was—

"Your one o'clock is here."

—disappearing as if by Doppler, slipping away.

•

In my office now, my self a thing in its proper place, the clock's hand quietly sweeping each moment under the rug of the next, my one o'clock was here, according to the voice on the intercom. Instead of immediately responding, I reread the printed email that I'd apparently neglected to take out of my pocket: *And I am imagining him exhaling that smoke, watching it float up lighter than air and then into her lungs, the ineffable made tangible, something that can stain, that lingered long after their lives diverged, in 1592.* Something now occurred to me, something new, that in Arolian we have no distinction between restrictive and nonrestrictive, so it must have been a choice here, to put that comma before the date, to restrict the act of divergence to a single occurrence. Without it, divergence would be recursive, a perpetual parting.

But that wasn't the thought of the hour, because my one o'clock was here: right here, in front of me, this couple whose names I had to retrieve from the slope of papers on my desk so many times they finally began, whenever I paused, just telling me their names—Aaron and Aline, or Erin and Alain, I couldn't keep them straight—and I said I was "going to ask you some questions that might at first seem intrusive, but this is a purely legal proceeding—by which I mean, it's both legalistic in nature and within the bounds of the law—and I am only asking such questions in order to verify the veracity of your relationship. Of course, the veracity of any relationship is always a question, even when you don't have to prove yourselves to someone like myself, but I just want to prepare you, rather I want you to prepare yourselves, for this line of questioning, prepare yourselves for this stranger in front of you to ask how often you make love, what sort of positions you prefer, what sort of—shall we say—proclivities the other harbors. Technically your answers themselves do not matter in determining the legitimacy of your alleged love—instead it's how your answers complement each other's that I am most interested in, but there are so many other ineffable factors that you must be aware of: inflections, gestures, pauses, factors I'm sure you're already aware of in some way, since they are factors that we all catalogue when we're with someone we care about, someone we hope cares equally for us, this hope being the impetus to investigate your lover's lag-time between your 'I love you' and theirs, to wonder why they close their eyes during coitus or why they still seem reluctant to pee with the door open. So this is really nothing new here. I just need to see that what you have is real, just as you need to see it every day, distilled into the tiniest gestures. Think of this as a mere rehearsal of those gestures. Go on. Gesture. Put your arms around each other. Please. Yes, that's it. Don't hesitate. Think how it must feel for the other right now, being on the receiving end of your affection's hesitations. Embrace one another, closer. There, yes, that's right, sit on his lap. It feels good, doesn't it. But don't look at me. Look at each other. I'm not here. Just—yes, that's it. See? Intimacy! Doesn't it feel good? This validation? But don't be so stilted with it. Here, the loveseat. Move over to the loveseat. It's more comfortable, more amenable. See? Wasn't I right? Now kick off those shoes."

•

And after Aaron or Alain stood up from the loveseat, leaned over my desk, and punched me square in the face; after I, eyes welling, pulled myself from the floor to find the couple gone, I was leaning over the hallway's drinking fountain, hoping for a cool stream of water to salve my swelling forehead and instead receiving a fierce jet of water straight to the pants, and I opened my eyes and saw, down the hall, near the entrance, that guy Gary talking to Patricia. That guy Gary served papers for the most popular divorce lawyer on the Island, a man whose mug smiled from every bus-stop bench around with a merkin-like soul-patch. That guy Gary was now asking Patricia where he could find Leonard Nist.

I slunk into the bathroom. The changing table, flopped down like a Murphy bed, was freshly smeared and had an eggy smell, and in the mirror I could see the welt from Aaron or Alain's knuckles starting to form above my brow.

I was pretty sure that guy Gary hadn't seen me but I couldn't risk going back out there now and letting him catch me, letting him hand over the document, letting him sound the death knell on my marriage. So I did the only thing a man of my education and sophistication could do in a situation like that. I climbed out the window. It was not a window for adults, not a wide berth through which a grown man could abscond with dignity. It made for a snug egress, and the ensuing escape required a fair amount of wriggling, squeezing, thinking thin. I finally emerged in the alley, scratched, missing a shoe, like a newborn, or maybe just a defenestrated man without a shoe.

•

I got in my car, searched the rearview and saw: that guy Gary leaving the ISNT office, checking his own reflection in the martinizer's mirrored window, sucking in his belly a bit, then getting into a green Rover.

I—the ringing in my ears like the slow deflating of a balloon between a child's pinched fingers, my head likewise soon to be a flaccid, saliva-slimed thing, discarded—drove back in the direction of the Hendricks-Kvint residence.

•

I was now driving back to Sou'est, with Pig in the passenger seat, having picked him up from the Madrid (Mel: "Where are you going?" Baxter: "Will you be back for dinner?"). Driving this part of the Island, it was impossible to feel like you were ever making much progress. The foliage that flanked the road was so thick, green, and unvarying, you felt like you were a Keystone Kop running in place while Mack Sennett churned a rotating background behind you, a cruel mockery of movement for the camera.

I kept an eye on my rearview, suddenly every vehicle a green Rover, that guy Gary incarnate in every motorist.

•

As I approached Alli and Grej's place, apartment number seven, accessible from the parking lot, I noticed the door was open, framing a scene of Alli unpacking groceries in an apartment furnished with moving boxes and dormlike depression. I tapped on the door with my wedding band.

"Hello," she said without looking up, stacking Stouffer's

into the freezer, an undefrosted ice-cave, a Fortress of Solitude for an action-figure Superman.

"May I come in?"

"In, in," she said in English. "Sorry, I'm Russian."

"What?"

"I said I'm Russian."

"I don't understand." Her file said she was born in the States. Was it possible that everyone was now revising the basics of their identity? "Your case file said you were born in the States."

"Excuse me?" She turned, brandishing a box of Lean Pockets. Dark hair pulled into a ponytail, her eyes smudged with mascara like a cat-burglar with an improvised mask. She was wearing Capri pants, or maybe ill-fitting boy's shorts. "What did you say?"

"Your file. It didn't say anything about Russia. Do you mean, like, culturally you're Russian?"

"I said, 'I am *rushing*.' I have to get to work in a few." She threw the Lean Pockets into the freezer. "If you're coming in, close the door behind you."

I stood in the middle of the seafloor-soft shag while she folded brown paper grocery bags. Each bag was painted with red perforated lines that would guide a child's safety scissors to cutting a spooky mask from it—not for Halloween but a reminder of the proliferation of costumes for the Tempest Fest.

After folding the bags, Alli piled them onto the counter, flat, where they began to slowly, Nosferatu-like, unflatten themselves.

"So," she said, retying her ponytail, tightening its facelift-effect on her features. "More rehearsals? Grej's not here."

"Why not? Where is he?"

"Do you ever just ask one question at a time?"

She walked over to the bed, or mattress rather, box-springless on the floor. From a duffel she pulled a polo shirt. "I don't know where he is. He was getting paranoid, said you'd been following us, looking into everything. He began throwing everything out. He hasn't shown up to work, and his boss called me, threatened to report him to The Truancy Bureau, would threaten our whole emigration."

"Truancy," I said. "Shit."

She stepped around me to get to the kitchen, where she emptied soda-browned water from a plastic cup, rinsed it out, filled it with tap.

"So I have no choice but to fill in for him."

She pulled on the maroon polo shirt and I caught a glimpse of the embroidered logo: BABY CAKES, the words written in frosting around a toroidal donut.

...

There once was an Islander, or so I'm told, who, generations ago, declared his home an independent sovereign state. His two-bedroom craftsman with foundation problems would from that day forward be its own nation, free to form its own governing bodies, collect taxes, create and enforce laws. It was unclear what this act of secession was in rebellion to; neighbors flipped through their mental Rolodexes for recently enacted laws from which the man might have been compelled to declare himself and his home free, but they could come up with none, unless he has been offended by the long-overdue repeal of the law that prohibited the washing of one's goat on a Sunday.

When his fellow Islanders asked this man about his new independence, they inevitably stumbled onto the problem of the name: if he was no longer Arolian, then what would he like to be called? How was the new nation-state of his house to be identified? The man—this potentate to a nation of one (for he had no family, and eventually the immigration laws he enacted between his home and the rest of the Island prevented him from acquiring any family)— was stumped. He had no idea what he should call his little fiefdom. Neighbors offered suggestions. Everyone was very helpful, for even those who were bewildered by his project still enjoyed the creative challenge of naming. But for every name they offered the man—this cluster of people standing there on the crabgrassed border—he swatted it down. All those names on offer, he told them, were relational: they depended on his being dependent on Arolia. No, it couldn't be North This or West That; he was looking for something not relational but essential. What, then, was essential about this place? He'd have to think on that. He could not finish the paperwork needed for complete sovereignty until he knew what to call this place, and per his own requirements that meant understanding its core nature, untethered from the onomastics of other geopolitical bodies. In the end, that essential nature remained unknown, and so it officially became Unknown.

...

She left for work on foot, and I spent a few minutes looking through my glove box for some loose papers with which to scrape a steamy new turd from the backseat. By the time I reduced the mess on the seat to a blurry brown smear, Alli was out of sight.

I drove to where I was pretty sure Baby Cakes was, and—after a detour through a part of Sou'est where I saw yellow crime scene tape cordoning off part of the sidewalk, a chalk outline that looked more Vorticist than forensic—found it, lit up and unearthly in a darkened neighborhood, every wall a window, as if the whole improbable place were simply a display. The fluorescent sign in the window, a donut with ALWAYS OPEN cursived neonly into the center hole, branded itself onto my retina.

•

Inside, Alli was behind the counter, and I salvoed with: "Why is it that donut shops are always open twenty-four hours a day?" I asked.

"Because," she said, "in a donut-shaped universe, time has no beginning or end."

"Is that right?"

"I don't know," she said. "On my shift a few nights ago, a physics professor came in, bought a bear claw, said something like that. Also said I reminded him of his daughter and tried to get my phone number."

"You've been covering for Grej for a few days now? When did he disappear?"

"Last week."

I'd seen him at the Tempest Fest only yesterday. But, more urgently: "May I use your facilities?"

She handed me the bathroom key, chained to a bicycle tire.

In the bathroom, the lights buzzed, flickered epileptically. The toilet was missing entirely. There was just a rust-rimmed absence. And yet, aside from that oversight, the bathroom's garishness tended toward the grandmotherly, not the gruesome: pink, honeycomb tiling, hexagonal patterns of grout, a new TP role with its end folded into a neat little chevron. The hand soap was scented of rosewater.

•

Five years ago, after the Paris trip, Grace and I stopped off in Rome on a daylong layover, popped into the Villa Borghese. Grace said Bernini's David looked like American actor Ray Liotta, then complained of stomach problems and excused herself to find a WC. She eventually caught back up with me in an overlit corner of Caravaggios, and her face was now pallid, sweaty, panickingly expressionless.

"Everything okay?"

"Fine, fine," she said.

Then, a couple rooms later, before a portrait of a woman the plaque insisted reflected Mannerism but I thought reflected fetal alcohol syndrome, she asked, "Do I stink?"

"Why?"

"Would you tell me if I did?"

"Why?"

"They didn't have a toilet seat. Didn't have a toilet, just a porcelain hole in the floor."

"Are you afraid you shat on yourself?"

"Shush!" Then she pretended to examine the profound use of positive and negative space, the brush strokes of genius. Around us people listened to audio tours, pressing plastic paddles to their ears.

"We need to leave," she whispered.

"You don't stink. You shit like a true Old-Worlder."

She relaxed a little, seemed to enjoy the colors and cracks of impressionist portraiture again, youth and age preserved together.

But I'd lied. She did stink. I spotted the ellipses of burnt sienna staining the back of her rabbit-tailed tennis socks. Behind her, people moved away. Standing beside my beshitted bride before the masterworks of the early modern, I congratulated myself, knew that if someone told me this anecdote in a status adjustment interview I'd note it as proof of selflessness (selflessness being number four on the checklist I'd inherited from my predecessor), proof that I was willing to ignore the stink of soiled socks in order to preserve my wife's self-respect. But just as an actor becomes aware that he's in a real, genuine moment—that he's experiencing something legit—only for that awareness to disintegrate the moment itself, I then wondered if in fact I was taking a bit too much pleasure in Grace's poopy sock.

She was, after all, always intimidatingly composed. I could only spot her Achilles heel when it was soiled brown. But no matter. I deferred to my original opinion, my professional opinion, stayed cozy in it.

•

At Baby Cake's front display counter—showing an assortment of diabetic wonders, everything glowing and glazed—Alli said, "You need to buy something."

"What?"

"The bathroom is for customers only. Technically, I should have made you buy something before you used it."

"Fine." I noticed her name tag: *Ich Bin Ein Berliner.* "I'll take a raspberry cruller."

I gave her fifty-nine cents and she handed me the knotted twist of sugary dough. I took a bite, allowed a moment for the sugar to metabolize. "I might have a lead on Grej."

She pushed herself up, grabbed a few moist towelettes from the dispenser behind the counter and handed them to me. "Here," she said. "Your hands, they're a mess."

"Did you hear me?"

"Best hold that thought, and go tend to your hog, Mr. Nist."

I turned. Outside, in the chiaroscuro of the donut shop's parking lot, in the back of my car, Pig was visible in the window, foaming at the mouth.

I ran outside, quickly discovered the foaming was simply foam, that Pig had begun gnawing on the seat stuffing. I opened the door. Pig was now burrowing further into the chewed-open upholstery, his instinct telling him to root for obscure French truffles but leading him to find only ossified French fries between the cushions. His head was down, rear up, presenting the asterisk of his asshole.

I scooted Pig out of the car, led him across the street to the little league field where the animal could work through his instincts.

I sat down, remained sitting even after the moisture of the grass made itself known, cool and dilating, through the seat of my pants.

I looked at the donut shop. I'd spent myself in the periphery of others' passions. I didn't belong here.

•

"You can't sleep here." It was Alli. She was standing over me, her shirt dusted with confectioner's sugar.

"I wasn't sleeping," I said. But of course I had been sleeping, for who-knows how long.

I got to my feet, brushed bits of grass from my shirt. The realization that Pig was no longer doing laps fibrillated my heart, until Alli touched me on the shoulder.

"He's okay. He's over there." She nodded toward the little league field's pitching mound, where Pig stood, having found the highest ground as if for a flood. He began gnawing on the rubber plate.

"I need to get him some food," I said. "You have a Pet Emporium around here?"

"I have some old dog-food at home," she said. "It's got anti-heartworm stuff in it, but I guess Pig could have it."

Above, the clouds, which during the day had been nacreous, furrowed as if by plow, were now making themselves known in the dark: a low-slung canopy of dirty dish-rags, aching to wring their gray water out.

"Why are you doing this?" she asked.

Which "this" did she mean? But I knew. "I saw him, yesterday," I said. "I can find him."

She said: "You better." A smirk pulled at the corner of her mouth like a fishhook. "The pig's coming home with me, and you're not getting him back until you do."

•

With dawn like a smear of sidewalk chalk, beneath clouds turned tumorous, I was driving again, sleepless save for the accidental snooze in the field.

Less familiar with Sou'est, I'd plugged the intersection of the Tempest Fest into the GPS on my dash, to navigate me back to familiar land, and I was now watching the screen, my blue-dot avatar moving obediently along the lighter blue line. From this imagined above, things were progressing simply, easily, as if on a predestined trajectory. Here I was, all my restless desires funnelled into a simple quest. Find Grej.

I must have been watching the screen when the car in front of me braked and I did not.

•

The ceiling of the ambulance, scored with scratches, was either slightly convex or slightly concave, flexing or folding. Couldn't be sure, as something gauzy covered my right eye, reducing all depth perception to guesswork, blind trust in the theory of a third-dimension.

I fingered the floss-enforced medical tape on the bridge of my nose, which, when I blinked, pulled at outlier eyebrow hairs.

The blurry face of an EMT hoved into view, began the interview.

Did I know my name? What year was it? Who was President?

Presumably I answered correctly, or correctly enough, as my slowly-coming-into-focus interviewer progressed to harder questions.

What was two plus two? When was five minus three? Why was one divided by two?

Just don't ask me the color of my wife's toothbrush.

Even if I did remember, during a years-ago hardware store debate over painting our bathroom either "Phosphene Green" or "Robotripping Red," Grace concluded that I was colorblind. She flipped through swatches of paint samples, holding them out like a courtesan's fan, or a poker hand whose secrets encoded doom. After that, she'd periodically ask, "What color do you think this is?" holding up a turquoise toque that might have actually been teal. I responded: "It doesn't matter. The word 'turquoise' has no intrinsic connection to the sensation of your eyes sending particular color signals to your brain." She cocked an eyebrow into a skeptical circumflex and smiled. Always playful, as if merely amused at the bumper-car confusion of my rods and cones, but still inviting me—teasingly, always teasingly—to doubt my grasp on the most fundamental of facts.

•

The EMT pointed a light into my eyes, sharp as a sniper's laser-sight. It somehow made visible for me the network of veins webbing the back of my eyeballs.

While my eyes recovered, the EMT's face remained a Van-Gogh swirl of Phosphene Green and Robotripping Red.

"Do you know where you are?" said this impressionistic blur, this approximation of a person.

"I'm going to the Tempest Fest." I tried to prop myself up, realized I was strapped down with industrial Velcro.

The EMT repeated his question. I repeated my answer.

"We're taking you to Memorial," he said.

"A memorial?" I had a sudden vision of my bronzed likeness above my freshly filled grave. The Island liked bronzing things. I'd always wanted to attend my own funeral.

"Not *a* memorial. Memorial General. The hospital."

•

Taking inventory of my body, starting by mentally fragmenting and intentionally *feeling* my constituent parts, then each part's constituent parts, from hand to finger to individual segments of phalange (just as the *sotto voce* of Grace's guided meditation CD implored her to do so many times as she sat butterfly-legged in our living room before the monoliths of our bought-hot stereo speakers), I was surprised that it all felt mostly okay, either in shock or sheer-luck health. Either way, I was relieved to be spared pain, for the time being. That was the real fear, not the injury but the pain, not the signal but the noise.

And then, as if hearing its cue: the pain arrived. There were points—at my shoulders, the crinkley base of my neck—epicenters, from which it spread, like a daub of ink soaking into paper, discovering its fibers, making them visible.

That's all pain was, I tried to convince myself, your body made visible to your brain, a reminder of its simple, dumb factness.

I said I needed to get to Tempest Fest.

"You're not the only one. That's what this traffic is all about. That American production just opened."

The EMT's face was now visible above me. He looked confident; he looked American. The man's jaw muscles were like wads of chew tucked into his cheeks, and likewise he seemed to speak through clenched teeth. "We've been stuck here hours. Driver left on foot. If you want, I can sedate you. Should last you until some of this has cleared."

•

I blinked, during which I had a dream of startling clarity, scenes with a depth of focus that defied the eyes' ability to triage detail, and when I opened my eyes, pulling myself out of sleep as if out of a tar pit, the EMT was curled motionless in the corner, head lolled against the wall, arms slack like Muppet limbs. I blinked again and time-traveled to the EMT rolling me out of the back of the ambulance. Like treading water, consciousness required continued effort.

I was in a wheelchair, though not at Memorial General. We were still on the side of the road.

It was now dusk, or dawn, some off-tone transitional state. With no knowledge of east and west, sunrise was the same as sunset; you just had to wait and see if the day was coming or going.

The traffic was everywhere, drivers either asleep at the wheel or absent, having, like our own driver, left on foot long ago.

The scene had a Pompeii quality to it, the sky dense with Vesuvian halitosis.

"Hospital is that way," the EMT said, pointing in a direction that looked utterly indistinguishable from all other directions: nubby trees sitting on the horizon like beads on an abacus, easily slid to any arbitrary point.

The EMT started wheeling me.

We went along the shoulder, where the concrete crumbled into dirt, where tectonic chunks of road seemed to be in the slow process of getting stolen away by errant gangs of wild grass.

The EMT was mumbling about wishing he had his motorcycle, that he could cut through this traffic if he did.

Something occurred to me, like a dead fish slapped across my face; that's what the inexplicable does: it just occurs. I asked, "What kind of music do you like?"

The EMT said, "Didn't peg you for a chatterer."

I had, however, pegged the EMT for a chatterer, and the man's sudden turn toward the taciturn—perhaps simple sleepiness—gave me a puppy-dog pang of neediness. "Have to pass the time somehow."

"Music," the man said, "all kinds. Except country and rap."

"I see."

In the distance, a flare of lightning did some awful violence to the sky.

I continued: "Favorite foods? Maybe a guilty-pleasure breakfast food? Cake, perhaps?"

A mile away, more, a wall of cloud, or just the amorphous substance of storm, was slowly absorbing all specificity of place. Trees, like twigs stuck in the ground, shivered, trying to wriggle free of the earth.

And then I heard it: the Aeolian Harp, that D minor ribboning through the air, weaving itself around the Island with harmonograph swirls. It was less a howling, as I remembered it from the last storm, more a mournful bellow, the wind pushing through the organ-stops of that headland's rock crevasse. I recalled in *The Tempest*

Ferdinand asking, "Where should this music be?" Indeed, it was everywhere, impossible to tell if the air was carrying the sound or the sound was moving the air. But then, as the wind calmed, so did the sound.

•

Most nights, Grace and I made things from things already made. Yesterday's bok choy, last week's broccoli rabe: fibrous stalks sautéed into digestibles. As a genre, it was less leftovers, more reappropriations, of things once thought forgotten at the back of the fridge into things we could finally forget.

After a stew, she once said, "We don't still have that dumpling squash, do we?"

"It was in here. We just ate it."

"Thank God, done with that carbuncular thing," scraping the uneaten into Tupperware for tomorrow's scramble.

The archaeology of every meal was complex, far-reaching, genealogical.

Generally speaking, we oiled things beyond recognition.

When she decided to go raw, my only recourse was to resign the kitchen to her. She produced things on platters, nuances of green surely unappreciated by the human retina, which produced in me inflations of angular gas. When I saw the vegetables again, they seemed no less recognizable, showed little effect for having passed through me, as if I were nothing, a simple conduit.

When beets came into season, with their blood-red

stool-staining properties, the toilet bowl daily prophesied doom—internal bleeding surely, some sort of hemorrhage, the end—until I remembered what I'd had for lunch, and felt reborn, signer of a new lease.

She wanted to know how it felt, the new pressing of nature. "We need to get back to it," she said. It felt good, I said.

And it did, this abrasion of health.

But the night before she left, I found in the kitchen junk drawer—amongst a few ineffectual knives still snotted with stale foodstuffs, ampersands of twist-ties, a couple dozen coupons—ketchup packets. High fructose corn syrup, red number five.

The ketchup packets reminded me of the guerilla theater I'd attempted as a kid: walking down a crowded sidewalk, lighting a firecracker out of sight, clutching my chest to burst a ketchup packet against my white shirt, collapsing to the ground in one last spasm of life, and then listening as the crowd around me dissolved into chaos and fear. I was usually resurrected—and my prank usually ruined—by my own fits of giggles, but, twenty years later, those plump little packets of condiment still had the look of squibs to me, of things just aching to go off, an event waiting to become itself.

•

By the time we got to the hospital, it was raining, but the air was too violent to respect the delicate integrity of a raindrop. Instead, the atmosphere was a tantrum of water molecules, hard and sharp and angry like sand in a sandstorm.

Stumps of signage, now decapitated, stuck in the ground.

The sky was darkly scalloped, something swirling behind the clouds like cream swizzled into coffee. Trying to move toward the hospital, we felt like hamsters who mistook the spin cycle for an exercise wheel. The ground was divotted, more: gouged and dug so deeply it was like a graveyard in which the interred had scheduled a walk-out.

As we got closer to the hospital, we joined the others trying to get in. They—these Tempest Fest attendees, survivors, presumably, of some opening night disaster— were bloodied, wound-shocked, casually dressed in injury like so many Halloween zombies.

We crossed the roundabout to the ER. Tempest Fest merch littered the asphalt, speckled with blood, other ambiguous materials.

It was now, most certainly, night.

•

In the ER, men of indeterminate injury and questionable equilibrium wandered to destinations uncertain, medical professionals pinging around in panic. The EMT wandered away, saying he'd be back in an instant. I found my phone in my pocket to discover I'd received a message from Penny saying she had Pig, saying some woman called her because it was her number on his tag, so now she had him.

Across the lobby, there by the minimalist painting on the wall that might have actually just been a frame someone neglected to fill, was a man whose slanted slouch, the back of his shirt showing a twisty rat's tail of hair, I knew instantly, though my rattled brain lagged in coming up with a name. A dilated, dream-like moment, knowledge without language. As soon as my brain did come up with a name, an identity—it's Grej, you idiot!—he was gone.

I grabbed the rubber-rimmed wheels and was off. Toward that empty frame, toward Grej. As I turned the corner, in hot pursuit, one wheel popped off the floor for an exhilarating moment—I had no idea I could get this thing going so fast! I was now in a hall, banked with elevators, three of which were closing. I wheeled toward them, saw one was headed to the third floor (*obstetrics*), one to the fifth floor (*podiatry*), one to the basement (*basement*). I tried to recall if Grej had ever mentioned a secret passion for birth medicine or foot doctoring. I recalled nothing of the sort, so in an elevator, I pushed the button for the basement.

When the doors opened curtain-like I saw two long rows of plastic trash bins, each marked with the medical waste logo, which on the Island is the image of Hermes's caduceus dripping blood.

Ours was a simple hospital, small and to the point. The basement itself was a corridor of damp cement walls, the ceiling a confusion of exposed piping.

I listened, heard only the dimmed bustle of the floor above. I wheeled myself between the rows of medical waste, smelled the used-BandAid musk creeping out. My wheels were squeaking.

"Grej?" I said, though it came out a whisper. I tried again. "Grej? Are you down here?" I heard only the parentheses of echoes around my words.

One trash bin I approached had its lid askew. The dark space between lid and bin bore all the bodily horrors that remained just beyond the event horizon of my consciousness. I felt faint just imagining what I could not fully imagine. Still, I inched toward it, just brain-bashed enough to be courageous, to have a look. I leaned forward in the chair, came closer to the ajar lid. In those few inches of darkness, something furry came into focus. What new sort of abjection was this? I couldn't stop my hand from pushing the lid a bit more, the blue light seeping in to show me not the terrifying possibilities of the human body but rather a slightly bloodied Caliban costume. Inside the bin, I recognized the familiar patches of toupees repurposed into fur, a result of the Island's hairpiece industry crashing a generation ago, its surplus a boon to the local theaters' costume designers. It was only then that I realized how bad the Tempest Fest riot had actually been—not from the damage to the people I'd seen but from the damage to the ephemera those bodies had shed. It was a grounding moment, a safe return from horror, back to props.

A flitter across my periphery. I thought I might have seen a body, the comet tail of a thin braid. I raced like, as the Americans say, the wind (as if they know what wind can really do).

I wheeled that way, found myself in the laundry. Large canvas dumpsters flowering over with sullied medical whites. Above each one was positioned a large aluminum shoot, from which the freshly used laundry would drop. As I wheeled, squeakily, down this hall, I heard four or five *whooshes* of new deposits dropping down from the hospital above. When I got to the end of the hall, I saw not a single person, just another corner, another turn: to a loading dock.

The concrete basement opened up into an absence big enough for a truck to back its load into. I pivoted in my chair, thinking Grej might have absconded via the truck route, when I heard a soft scramble behind me, turned to see a body fumbling out of a laundry basket, running off, away.

"Grej!"

I grabbed my wheels, wheeled.

This able body was faster than me, and he was soon out of sight. But I followed the patter of his feet to the stairwell, frustratingly far from the elevators.

Those stairs, they looked as surmountable as the side of a skyscraper. I pushed myself to my feet and raced up the stairs. I couldn't understand the stair's inability to stay true, their tendency to distort, dilate and contract, but I managed to stay on my feet until I got to the door at the top.

I burst through, lights like a splash of cold water.

In the glutted hospital lobby again, my legs gave out. The linoleum felt even more concussing than the crash.

•

The EMT was now back on stage, leaning over me, hands on knees, his.

174

He exhaled, nose-hairs aquiver. He opened his mouth to speak but said only, "You know." From below, I could see that the EMT had had either extensive cavity fillings or recently eaten an Oreo. Judging from the flavor of his halitosis, the latter. I wondered if the EMT was going to offer me one.

Instead, the man said, "She left. She flew to her aunt's."

"You *are* Cake4Breakfast."

He pointed to—tapped, really, as if to simply show his dirty, deckle-edge fingernail—a patch on his lapel, a name embroidered in nostalgic cursive, one of those names that looked familiar enough, with a standard framing of consonants, but also, at closer glance, a three-card-monty rearrangement of vowels, a remix of a name that would always sound, or be, mispronounced. "You're not very observant," said the newly named man.

•

Grace going to her aunt's meant Grace going to Iceland. That's where Grace's aunt had gone, making good on that promise. Must have been about ten years ago, as she'd come to the wedding flushed with excitement for the move, steering every conversation, non-sequiturally, to dead-end into Iceland, crash against its shores. At the reception, she'd dashed off Icelandic facts more fitting a grade-school social studies report: main export (fish, aluminum, elfin pop music) and national bird (something called a gyrfalcon, which sounded like a mythical mashup, a Dr. Moreau creation that should not be but, in impossible Iceland, was).

I'd never actually been to that little isle of Viking false advertising, but I'd seen the photos of our neighbor to the north on the aunt's latest social media blitz, all those alien calcifications of earth, hot springs seen in the distance like the steam-filled earth had sprung a leak. Those photos were fisheyed to fit it all in, so fisheyed, in fact, the convexity of the images seemed to simulate the curve of the earth, as if up there, so close to the top, the overwhelming cosmic truths were suddenly visible to the plain eye.

...

There once was an Island, or so I'm told, an island that once was described in the 1832 book *A Narrative of Four Voyages*, by the American Benjamin Morrell, as having the "qualities of an Aeolian Harp, as if the whole pile of rock were animated to sing when a fierce air coursed over it, or maybe through it." This was the only northern Atlantic island mentioned in the book, and Morrell never provided coordinates. After leaving this unnamed island, Morrell, in the ship the *Wasp*, ventured south, to a landmass he named New South Greenland, down near the Antarctic's Weddell Sea. Of this taut archipelago Mr. Morrell gave specific coordinates and descriptions clearly designed with future cartographers in mind, and in 1912, around the time that nine thousand miles north, the *Titanic* was passing by Arolia without even as much as a horn-toot of acknowledgement, the German explorer Wilhelm Filchner was attempting to confirm Morrell's claims and coordinates of New South Greenland; he found nothing but water, and a few years later Ernest Shackleton, captaining the *Endurance*, confirmed Filchner's suspicions, that the island Morrell described simply did not exist. It was perhaps the specificity of Morrell's recordings of New South Greenland that drew its existence into doubt, as the vague lyricism with which he briefly described that other island, the one with "qualities of an Aeolian Harp," never seemed to have lured the confirmation-hungry Mr. Filchner.

Benjamin Morrell's motivation for such a deception could only be guessed, and the writings of this confirmed fabulist were—and are—looked at as nothing more than a compendium of imaginary lands.

There once was an Island, or so I'm told.

...

When I got to Iceland, I told myself, I would find Grace's aunt's house, would knock on the door and Grace would answer and I would say something that would convince her to fly back to the Island with me. I'd return to the Madrid and collect my things, bid farewell to Baxter and Mel, who, in my absence, would have outfitted the room like a soundstage for their increasingly popular Internet fuck vids. "We have a responsibility to our fans," Mel would say, adjusting a softbox light, "a responsibility of excellence," then nibble away at a cuticle, a fleck of glossy purple fingernail paint left on her lip.

I would visit my predecessor, at Sunrise Retirement Community, approach him there in the rec room's sun patio, this man all liver-spotted, hair gone gossamer, staring in the direction of the tree-filled valley but his eyes nearsightedly jumping from dust mote to dust mote, this man who'd retired to tend to the particular mythos of his own dementia. I would sit beside the man, explain that I'm quitting. My predecessor would turn to me, irises smoked behind cataracts, gesture to me a flourishy something, fingers arthritically bent, communicating nothing, and then quietly soil himself.

I would then drive to Penny's, retrieve Pig. "Good," Penny would say, "he needs a strong male presence." Penny, corkscrewed into her bean bag chair, which would have sprung a leak and be dribbling a bland confetti of white dots all over the floor, would make her mouth like a flutist's to blow the steam off her mug of tea. But I would have decided that Pig needed a suitable home, one where he wasn't a practice child or a stand-in or an overburdened metaphor but a simple pig, irreducible, and so I would take him back to Pet Emporium and fill out a Pet Adoption card. And then one day, I'd get a call and then a ring at the door—because of course by this point Grace and I would be living in some sort of comfortable house-type situation with a doorbell—and a teenager would be there, a kid, wiry limbs scabby from skateboarding and completely reptiled with overlapping tattoos, an apprentice maybe. He'd say he was here for the pig.

But, before all that, I would first have to land in Iceland, find Grace's aunt's house, find another place I did not belong, and knock on the door. And, hopefully, Grace would answer, and she would probably be wearing that cardigan, the green one gone lacy from moth-bites and wear. She would smile, then let the smile fade into a squint against the sun. This sun, it would be dim but coming at us from everywhere, diffused by clouds cumulus and almost brainy, and so I'd keep talking, talking, about Pig, reuniting with him and recovering him from Penny, about my life at the Madrid with Baxter and Mel, about the fire, news of which would shock her, because of course she hadn't done it, because shit just had a way of happening like that, becauses symmetry capsizes and meaning drowns. I'd do my best to outline for her a Grace-shaped void, the vacuum that would pull her back in, and she'd have that just-woken tabula-rasa look, eyebrows unmade and unexpressive, not yet fixed against the world, not yet readable. And then she would speak: she would say something that I could not possibly anticipate.

•

And before that, I'd have to find my way to a plane, a red eye, as she had, find my way off the Island, find my way to a window seat to watch the shrinking stitchwork of light as we gained altitude. I would, as she had, watch, through the plane's oval portal window, the wing's metal paneling start shuffling, then reverse, rearrange itself. The jets whirring, preparing the air, the propulsive breath of vacuums powerful enough to pull themselves into, an insatiability of negative space.

•

Ten years ago, after I dropped the match into the gasoline outside the abandoned barn, Grace and I stepped back and she grabbed my hand. Together we watched that blue flame rush wavelike into the barn where it disappeared for a moment before reappearing all around the foundation, as if that small cardboard-box of a building could have been borne into the air on a bed of fire.

•

Below me would be the coast: waves more detonative than wavelike. And there, at the end of the beach, would be the Aeolian Harp: that giant wall of stone through which this air was coursing. Between ocean and rock, the earth prostrated itself then peeled back like flesh from bone, to reveal the awesome stone base of the Harp.

From above, I'd be able to look down on all this—this hospital, these people, this body—as the sound completely took over, and I'd get to watch all those structures down there doing their feeble best against the wind, creaking and groaning—more: like bones slowly breaking—as that D-minor coursing through the rock was once again becoming the sole force of nature, testing this structure's claim not just to stability but to sheer physicality. And as the ceiling flew away, ascending into a sky gone mad, all those images down there would be rendered spirit-hazy, those tiny figures like actors in a fade-out, as the air lifted them, the bodies, pulling them into the sound, before the vision dissolved.

For their help and support,

I'm grateful to Diana Thow,

Peggy Thow,

Anita Allardice,

and Christopher Tilghman,

in whose workshop this novel began.

KEVIN ALLARDICE is the author of two previous novels: *Any Resemblance to Actual Persons* (Counterpoint, 2013) and *Family, Genus, Species* (Outpost19, 2017). He lives with his wife, the translator Diana Thow, and their son in the San Francisco Bay Area, where he teaches high school.

Made in the USA
Monee, IL
31 January 2022